"You never talk about it."

Connor made a noise between an exhale and a groan as he took the seat next to her. "What?"

"The years before you met me."

He balanced his elbows on his knees and let his hands hang down between his legs. A thumb rubbed along the calloused palm of his other hand. "They don't matter."

The temptation to reach out and skim her fingers down his back kicked strong. The months apart had taken a toll on Jana. She missed holding him, making love with him. The simple things like cooking breakfast together and laughing over a movie.

Sitting close, smelling his familiar scent, brought it all rushing back in a punch of longing so powerful she almost doubled over from the force of it. But she forced her mind to hold on to the conversation and his voice to remain steady. "Because?"

"I didn't have you."

TRACELESS

HELENKAY DIMON

Recycling programs for this product may not exist in your area.

To Michelle Gorman—this one's for you!

ISBN-13: 978-0-373-69765-6

TRACELESS

This edition published by arrangement with Harlequin Books S.A.

For questions and comments about the quality of this book, please contact us at CustomerService@Harlequin.com.

Printed in U.S.A.

ABOUT THE AUTHOR

Award-winning author HelenKay Dimon spent twelve years in the most unromantic career ever—divorce lawyer. After dedicating all that effort to helping people terminate relationships, she is thrilled to deal in happy endings and write romance novels for a living. Now her days are filled with gardening, writing, reading and spending time with her family in and around San Diego. HelenKay loves hearing from readers, so stop by her website, www.helenkaydimon.com, and say hello.

Books by HelenKay Dimon

HARLEQUIN INTRIGUE

1196—UNDER THE GUN*
1214—NIGHT MOVES
1254—GUNS AND THE GIRL NEXT DOOR*
1260—GUNNING FOR TROUBLE*
1297—LOCKED AND LOADED*
1303—THE BIG GUNS*
1352—WHEN SHE WASN'T LOOKING
1369—COPY THAT
1387—SWITCHED
1434—FEARLESS**
1440—RUTHLESS**
1488—RELENTLESS**
1493—LAWLESS**
1498—TRACELESS**

*Mystery Men
**Corcoran Team

CAST OF CHARACTERS

***Connor Bowen*—**He's the leader of the Corcoran Team. He runs undercover operations, plans rescue missions and protects for a living, but he can't figure out how to win his estranged wife back.

***Jana Bowen*—**Jana left the security of her Annapolis home to clear her head. Being married to a man who puts himself in danger on a daily basis is one thing, but the security measures he insists she live by are strangling her. She loves him but worries she won't be able to get him to listen...then the attackers come and all she can think about is getting back to Connor.

***Marcel Lampari*—**The executive director of the charity where Jana used to work offers her a refuge when her relationship with Connor falls apart, but doing so raises Connor's ire. In helping Jana, Marcel steps right into the middle of her marriage, which may just be what he had planned all along.

***Luc Pearson*—**Luc's task is supposed to be easy: get the woman, make her cough up whatever information she has, then move on. But nothing is going according to plan. Not when he's lost sight of who's in control.

***Rich Stapleton*—**He's supposed to be a yes-man. A gun-for-hire and nothing else, but his hot head and all those questions could blow the whole deal.

***Bruce Harding*—**He is the outside man. The one hired by a mysterious boss to grab Jana. He doesn't say much, but that doesn't make him any less deadly. The question is, when everything goes haywire, which side will he stand on?

***Drake Federson*—**Drake was once Connor's mentor and comes running when Connor calls. He's got skills and has a history with the charity Jana works for. He seems too good to be true.... Is he?

***Holt Kingston*—**The leader of the Corcoran Traveling Team and a man Connor depends on for backup. He lands in Utah expecting to help Connor find his wife, but the mission blows up into so much more.

Chapter One

Jana Bowen looked at the numbers again. The black ink blurred and she rubbed her eyes to bring the columns back into focus. When that failed she leaned back in her metal desk chair and ignored the groan of the rusted back legs.

The charity didn't have a lot of money and prided itself on using a low percentage of the donations for administrative costs. Still, if her butt inched any closer to the floor her backache would become permanent. She vowed to head out tomorrow and find a new chair somewhere in the desert of Southern Utah.

With the scaling red rocks and miles of untouched land, this area of land on the edge of Zion National Park near the border of Arizona possessed a raw beauty. She'd ventured here, far from the calm of her historic Annapolis home, in search of peace.

Hooking back up with her former employer, Boundless Global, she spent her days running education programs and arranging for the shipment of vaccines to countries in desperate need of them. Getting lost in the mess in the office files the first day, she now spent her extra hours cleaning up paperwork. The work provided a needed distraction from her train wreck of a marriage and the man she missed more than she ever thought possible.

But right now she had a bigger puzzle on her hands

than Connor Bowen. She turned to the charity's executive director and her friend of many years, Marcel Lampari. "The paperwork isn't matching up."

"Still too many boxes?" He stood on the other side of the open main room lined with tables and covered on every surface with boxes and paperwork.

The building they used for their headquarters had been designed as a chapel decades before. Abandoned and far from anything other than brush and the rock canyons nearby, the four-room structure was donated to Boundless and quickly restructured to fit desks with computers and the command center for U.S. operations. The vast majority of the staff worked in countries receiving aid. Only Marcel and a few full-time employees worked from here, overseeing donations, a large group of volunteers and distribution chains. With her stepping in, that made four of them in the church office on a regular basis.

She took on the tasks of matching up shipping manifests and double-checking invoices after her initial review and filing led to inconsistencies. Marcel didn't have the time, and the staff member assigned to the job had relocated to another state, leaving the position in limbo until someone permanent could be hired.

It was mind-numbing monotony that filled the void. Or that was the theory. Since leaving Connor she'd found nothing eased the pain of missing him.

She concentrated on numbers and information contained in boxes on a form in front of her but the math just didn't work. "I'm up to three mistakes in the Nigeria shipments."

This couldn't be a simple math error. After getting an anonymous email from someone in the distribution chain, she'd begun poring through the files. Every third shipment was off. Exactly the third shipment and by exactly four crates. The paperwork at the receiving end didn't match the shipping information and the mysterious boxes disappeared as strangely as they had appeared.

"Maybe the trucking company is piggybacking someone else's shipment on ours then offloading it." Marcel tucked the pen behind his ear as he always did and flipped through the documents on his clipboard.

She doubted Marcel's explanation but she went along because it was easier than thinking about a worst-case scenario—one where someone was playing with the shipments. "I'd like to think people wouldn't cheat a charity."

"Let's not panic." He walked over and stood on the opposite side of her small desk. "It could just be that someone can't add."

"It's possible, but over and over?"

He made a face and pretended to count on his fingers. "Numbers are hard."

She had to laugh at that. "Yeah, I guess so."

Marcel didn't ruffle. It was one of the things she admired about him. In his late forties, his hair had long ago gone salt and pepper. He was long and lean and the perfect mentor, having spent most of his life in war-torn areas. She admired his dedication and ached for him over the recent loss of his wife of more than twenty years in a horrible car accident.

In his grief, he dove into his work. When Jana's life fell apart seven months ago from Connor's mix of smothering protection and workaholic tendencies, she showed up unannounced on Marcel's doorstep. He let her stay, because who could turn down free labor? She guessed he also recognized a fellow damaged person when he saw one.

"Why don't you get some rest? We can figure this out tomorrow." He dropped his clipboard on top of the stack of files in front of her. "We'll call around and get some answers."

Not the most subtle it's-time-to-head-out signal, so she got the message. "You're right."

"Let's go." He snapped his fingers. Probably being one of the few men who could do it and get away with it. Had something to do with his slight French accent from his childhood and the soft delivery.

"I have to lock everything up." She turned to the side and tapped the top of the safe. "I'll head out in a second."

He frowned at her. "A windstorm is kicking up, so don't wait too long."

She glanced at her watch. "Ten more minutes."

By the time she looked up again, night had fallen and the sky outside the window across from her was dark. The wind rattled the old building and whistled through the beams. She winced as she calculated whether she'd missed her opportunity to get back to the garage-turned-bunkhouse for the workers.

The banging started a second later. A fist pounding and the faint sound of a male voice.

She got up. "Marcel?"

The door slammed open before she made it to the other side of her desk. The song she'd been humming screeched to a halt in her head and a wave of panic washed over her as two men dressed all in black burst inside. The last of her reality jumbled as her gaze slipped from the masks that hid all but their eyes to the guns in their hands.

Glass shattered somewhere behind her. Between the crashing and unexpected sight in front of her, her legs refused to move. Everything passed in slow motion and she kept blinking, convinced she'd slipped into a weird nightmare.

When one of the men rushed toward her, she forced the

air back in her lungs and her brain jumpstarted. She spun around, thinking to get to the emergency door at the back of the building and run screaming for help. Her hip hit the edge of the desk and something crunched under her foot, but she stayed upright. Adrenaline fueled her run as she raced through the maze of desks, ducking and zigzagging despite the small space. Anything to make it harder for the men to shoot at her.

Glancing over her shoulder, she saw them behind her, walking slow and steady now but gaining ground with each long step. Their calm refused to register in her head. Their actions made no sense. Neither did the papers flying around the room and the sudden brush of air over her skin.

As she blew past each table, she grabbed for the boxes and phones and threw anything she could touch on the floor behind her to block the attackers' path. The thump of packages hitting the floor echoed around her as she folded an arm over her head and plowed forward. The thud of boots on the hardwood grew closer as her breath caught in her throat.

Almost there. She skidded around the long desk near the back of the room and slammed into a file cabinet. Her body was a mass of bumps and bruises but she pushed through, barely feeling anything except the driving need to get to the back door.

She slipped into the small hallway at the far end of the main room and plunged into darkness. The light should be on but the usual hum was gone as she felt her way along the wall. Finally, her hands hit the bar running across the middle of the back door and she shoved with all her might.

The whir of the alarm spun around her as the warm air hit her face. Without houses and street lights, the night was lit only by a blanket of stars. In two steps, she walked into the path of the motion sensor and the floodlights clicked on.

Her sneakers slid on the dirt and pebbles beneath her feet. Her chest rose and fell in hard breaths as she looked at the semicircle of men standing outside the back door. Four of them, all dressed like their friends who were now moving up behind her and pushing her forward without touching her.

Now locked outside and surrounded, she stared at the line of quiet men, including the two pointing guns right at her. One broke away from the group and closed the distance. As he did, the men following her drew even with her and took off their masks. She knew what letting her see their faces meant—she didn't stand a chance. They couldn't leave behind a witness.

Terror surged around her and thickened the air. Choking and gasping, she backed up but a hand landed between her shoulder blades and shoved her forward again.

The man glanced to his right. "Kill the alarm."

"What do you want?" When he faced her again her voice shook as she fought to keep the fear trembling through her from knocking her to the hard ground.

"You." A single word said in a slight accent.

Even in her haze it sounded wrong, almost forced. Before she could say anything else, the man reached out and grabbed the side of her neck. His fingers tightened in a squeeze that dug into her flesh and brought tears to her eyes. She bent over and tried to push him away. But he didn't stop until she was on her knees in front of him.

Panting and rubbing the throbbing pain running into her shoulder, she looked up, trying to make out the man under the mask. "There isn't any money here."

He crouched down until his face hovered in front of her and his dark eyes bored into her. "I don't want money."

She balled her hands into fists and tried to call up every self-defense strategy Connor ever taught her. Running meant potentially running into a man with a gun, or at best, heading into unknown darkness.

But she could stall. "We don't have medicine or vaccines."

"I don't care."

The horrors of what that could mean played in her mind. She pushed out the violent images in the hope of staying sane.

The alarm cut off. Only the sound of her labored breathing filled her ears. She filled the silence with babble, hoping a plan would pop into her mind. "You're in the wrong place."

"No, Jana Bowen, I'm not."

Like that, her muscles went slack and her mind went blank again. "You know me?"

She'd been in near hiding since she got there, not venturing out and only calling Connor at prearranged check-in times. The idea of someone tracking her down sent a new shock of fear spiraling through her.

"I want your husband."

"This is about Connor?" It was his greatest worry come to life. The reason he gave for keeping her in a near lockdown for the five months before she left home. He stressed her safety until it smothered everything else and strained their marriage.

"Your husband and I have some unfinished business."

"But we're separated." Through it all, it hurt to say the words. She never spoke them out loud, but if these men wanted Connor, she wanted Connor to stay away. And she would do anything, say anything, to make that happen.

The man grabbed her chin and forced her head up higher. "Connor will come for you."

She tried to shake loose of her attacker's hold but he only tightened his grip. "You don't understand. We're not together."

"As soon as he gets my message, he'll call." The man shoved her away, sending her falling on her backside in the dirt. "Then the fun can begin."

CONNOR FROZE WHEN he heard the doorbell. Sometimes he forgot he even had one of those.

He glanced around the open room with its conference room table and rows of computer monitors, and desks, and walls lined with secure filing cabinets. Keeping in his seat at the main terminal, he reached over and tapped the code into the small gun safe under the desk. There were others in the house, but this one was closest.

Except for the kitchen and a small living room, most of the bottom floor of the three-story brick house served as Maryland headquarters for the Corcoran Team, the private security company he owned. They specialized in risk assessments and high-priority but under-the-radar kidnap and rescue missions. Working off the grid meant deep cover, which also meant he didn't exactly hand out his address.

He certainly never got unexpected guests around midnight.

He got up as the doorbell rang a second time. One tap of the keyboard and the large screen mounted on the wall flickered on. The alarm system feed showed images from every camera outside the house. Someone with a baseball cap pulled low stood on the front porch holding what looked like an envelope and shifting his weight from foot to foot.

The unwanted visitor was enough to get Connor moving. He slipped around the conference table and headed for the foyer. Cameron Roth, a member of Corcoran's traveling team, met him at the bottom of the stairs. He was spending a few nights in the crash pad on the third floor, but right now he waited, fully dressed, with a gun in his hand.

"What's going on?" Cam asked.

"No idea."

"I'll handle backup." Cam took the last few steps and set up position flat against the wall on one side of the door. "You get to be the target."

Connor tucked his gun at the back of his waistband. He had another by his ankle and Cam as insurance, so Connor felt safe unlocking and opening the door.

He caught the guy halfway down the front steps on the way back to the beat-up sedan idling by the sidewalk. "What do you want?"

The guy jumped then spun around. Make that a kid. The tall, all limbs and no coordination type. He was fidgety and had the eye-darting thing down.

"I have a package," the kid sputtered.

"At midnight?"

"I got extra to bring it now. Are you Connor Bowen?" When Connor stayed silent, the kid practically threw the padded envelope at him. "I had to wait three extra hours to deliver it as ordered. The guy said it was pretty important and said you'd be the one to answer."

The timing and delivery didn't make much sense, but Connor—and Corcoran—had a lot of enemies. It was entirely possible that one of them planned on crawling right up his lawn, or at least wanted to send a message that he could.

Connor was not in the mood to play. "Who? I want a name."

The kid visibly swallowed and started backing down the stairs. "I don't have one."

"Then who do you work for?" Cam stepped into the doorway, not bothering to hide the gun in the hand hanging by his side.

The kid's eyes almost popped out of his head. He took another step and almost went down when his heel overturned. "Whoa, what are you—"

"Stop." Connor didn't yell but the kid stilled anyway. "Now answer the question."

"I had instructions." Words rushed out of the kid as he held up his hands. "All the information about my boss is on the packing slip. You can ask him. I just needed the money for, you know, stuff this summer."

Connor swore. "Unbelievable."

"You should leave." Cam waved the kid away. "And stop going to strangers' houses at midnight."

Connor heard the slap of sneakers against the pavement followed a minute later by the rev of a car engine. None of which grabbed his attention. Curiosity nailed him. He didn't even wait for the door to close to check the package. Taking it back into the office, he had a pair of gloves on and went to work.

A few seconds later Cam appeared on the other side of the conference table. He watched the preliminaries with a frown. "Paranoid much?"

"It's protocol." The package could contain a host of dangers and Connor was already breaking rules to rip it open fast. "And do you blame me in light of some of the people we handle?"

"Good point."

Wearing the blue gloves, Connor ran his hand over it, carefully squeezing. "Feels empty."

"Want to x-ray it?"

The question highlighted the step Connor decided to skip. One of them. "No time."

"How do you know that?"

"I'm not sure." But the churning in his stomach and twitching at the back of his neck gave him the clues. His instincts shouted at him to hurry.

Sliding a letter opener under the flap, Connor broke the seal. He upended it onto the paper Cam spread out on the conference room table. A ring bounced around on the table, pinging and spinning. Gold and slim.

With each rotation the anxiety built in Connor. He slammed a palm against it to stop the noise then picked it up. He didn't know anything about jewelry but he recognized this. To be sure, he tilted it to get a better look at the inscription and read the piece of the Aristotle quote.

"A single soul inhabiting two bodies..."

Cam leaned in and studied the ring. When he straightened again, the frown morphed into a look of confusion. "I don't get it."

Connor did. The kick to his gut had him rubbing a hand over his stomach from the sharp whack of pain there. "It's Jana's."

The phone he always carried with him buzzed in his pocket. It couldn't be a coincidence his wife's wedding ring arrived right as the private line only she knew about lit up. He braced his body for the killing blow.

If this was the way she planned to tell him their temporary separation had become permanent in her mind, she could forget it. He was not losing her. He'd get on a plane and fly to her. No more waiting or giving her space.

She asked and he obliged, even though every day without her sucked a piece of his soul away. But the end? No way. Wasn't happening.

Feeling the heat of Cam's stare and tension coiling inside, Connor slid his thumb across the screen and lifted the phone to his ear. "Jana?"

"No, but she says hello."

The metallic twinge had Connor's head snapping back. He recognized a voice modifier. More out of habit and training than actual thought, he pressed the speaker button.

Jana's voice filled the room. "Connor, stay away!" The tremble gave way to a scream then all sound cut off.

"Jana!" Connor almost dropped the phone as adrenaline and anxiety thundered together in his brain.

The other voice filled the line again. "She's done talking."

The word *done* echoed in Connor's head. "Where is she? Put her back on."

"That's enough." The modifier only highlighted the menace in the person's voice. "This isn't a negotiation. You have your proof of life."

"Who is this?" Connor could barely get the question out.

This time the voice laughed. "The man holding your wife. And if you want her back, you'd better get smart fast and figure out where she is."

"What are you talking about?"

"You have seven hours and a long way to travel."

The line cut out but Connor kept yelling over the buzzing sound in his ear. "Wait, where are you?"

"Okay." The color drained from Cam's face as he blew out a breath. "Any idea who that was?"

With a shaking hand, Connor hit the end button and fought off the mix of panic and fury whipping through him. "The man who kidnapped my wife."

Chapter Two

The noises in Jana's head roared, growing louder with each second until she woke with a start. She tried to move her arms and something pinched her stomach. She tugged again and bindings dug into her skin.

She bit back a scream as she opened her eyes. Blinking, she adjusted to the pale light and tried not to draw any attention or move her head as she glanced at the area right in front of her and just off to the sides. She couldn't turn around and see behind her, but she picked up enough clues to know she'd been moved.

A small room with a few windows. No furniture except the rickety, hard chair under her. A wood floor thick with dust. And two bruisers dressed in black, standing on either side of a window next to what she assumed was the front door to this cabin. Without facing her, they looked like the same ones who burst through the door back at the office.

The pieces didn't add up to anything good.

She searched her memory for a building that fit what she saw and remembered an abandoned shack about two miles from the charity. She'd found it while out walking one day, trying to clear her head and work through the pain of not being near Connor.

Connor… Because of her he would walk into a trap. She closed her eyes on the wave of pain that crashed over her.

"The princess is awake."

At the sound of the male voice her eyes popped open again. Her captor, the one who had hovered over her earlier while he threatened Connor over the phone, stood right over her again. There still was nothing hiding his identity, which confirmed they did not plan for her to survive whatever they were plotting.

He or one of these guys must have knocked her out. Some way she'd ended up here with only these three. She had no idea how many hours had passed but could see from the area outside the window that it was dark outside. The sky took on an eerie gray and tall trees blocked her view of anything more than a few feet away from the building.

Hoping to stall, do anything to get her bearings again, she said the first thing that came into her head. "How is Connor supposed to find me here?"

The man she thought of as the leader shrugged. "He's resourceful."

"He's not superhuman." But he was close. He'd saved her from an impossible situation once before and she had to believe he would somehow do it again. But at what cost?

When he received the call he'd sat hours away in Maryland. There was no way he could catch a commercial flight at that hour. But he was ingenious. He knew people. He never spoke about his time before starting the Corcoran Team or whatever he did years ago in black ops, but it conditioned him for situations like this. She knew that much.

The leader crouched down and met her at eye level. "I am well familiar with your husband."

"How?" Because if he knew Connor from the old days, this guy might have the same skills and then… She couldn't think about the "then" part.

"You don't need to worry about that now."

"He won't get here in time." Even if he did land in Utah

by the deadline, she had no idea how he would know where to look for her.

Shifting her shoulders, she tried to move her hands but they stayed locked behind her. There was a little give in the ropes binding her ankles, but too much shifting and the chair would tip over. She didn't see how that would help her.

She concentrated, trying to figure out if she still had her phone, but the ties lay flat and tight against her body and she didn't see any signs of bulging from the cell. That was really bad news since her phone had a chip in it and could provide Connor with a beacon to find her.

The idea had been for Connor to know her location at all times. He insisted it was a matter of safety, not trust. Before she left home she viewed it as further evidence of his overzealous need to wrap her up and store her away.

All that had changed now. The chip, the constant analysis, his insistence she run recovery drills with the team struck her as sound planning. The ability to commandeer a flight in record time might turn out to be the perfect trait in a husband.

"For your sake, let's hope you're wrong about your husband's tardiness." The leader stood up but stayed bent over her. His mouth loomed close to her ear. "And stop fidgeting."

"You think I'm going to sit here for hours and wait to die?"

He balanced his hands on his thighs and continued to lean in close. "Would you rather be unconscious? Because I could arrange that. Again."

Footsteps clomped against the hardwood right before a second man appeared at the leader's side. This was one of the guys who chased her through the charity building. "Or I can keep you occupied."

Her stomach flipped as bile rushed up her throat. This

one, taller and bulkier, wore a feral grin. His gaze never stopped roaming and the heat in his eyes promised pain.

The leader chuckled as he stood up and slapped the other man on the back. "Looks like my associate here is eager to step in and keep you company as you wait."

"Yeah, I am. She ran last time. She won't this time." The guy reached out and the tips of his fingers touched her hair.

She flinched and threw her body in the opposite direction. "Don't touch me."

The chair rocked and teetered. She would have crashed to the floor, unable to brace for the impact, if the leader hadn't clamped a hand down on her shoulder and steadied her.

He smiled at his friend. "It would appear she's not interested."

Fear pumped through her. Every bone shook and she fought to keep the tremor out of her voice. Panic and revulsion mixed until her head pounded. "No."

"Are you sure?" This time the oversized attacker grabbed her hair. Balled it in his fist and pulled. "You must be lonely if you and your husband are really separated."

The leader's eyebrow lifted. "Well, Jana? Is he right? Are you looking for someone to keep you busy and your mind off your husband?"

Tears came to her eyes as the man ripped strands of hair from her head. She stopped moving—anything to keep him from getting a tighter grip. From pulling her closer to him or his hot breath blowing cross her cheek.

She inhaled through her nose, desperate to calm the nerves jumping around inside her. Tried to remember all of Connor's instructions and the directions he called out during his impromptu safety drills. The most basic was to keep the attackers talking. Make them deal with her as a human being and not a product to be traded. "Tell me why you want Connor."

The leader shrugged. "Tell me why you don't."

"He will kill you both when he gets here."

The men looked at each other and laughed. The one with the death grip on her hair spoke up. "I doubt that."

"Let me go."

"That's enough." The leader pushed his friend back and crowded her.

She could smell the sweat on his skin and the heat pouring off him through his clothes. She fought to keep the dizziness from knocking her over as terror ran wild through her. "What are you—"

"Quiet or I will put one in your mouth, too." A black slip of material dropped out of the leader's hand and he waved it in front of her face. He came at her with his hands out. His thigh touched against hers as he practically stood on top of her.

"No." She shook her head, swiveled and turned.

He grabbed her chin in a bruising hold. "Stop."

When he slipped the material over her eyes, the room went black. She couldn't make out shadows. Nothing. Terror gripped her in the darkness. Fear like she'd never known crashed over her as she gasped for breath.

Her panic only made the leader angrier. His motions turned jerky and more forceful. He tied the knot behind her head and pulled tight, causing pain to spread through the back of her head.

"Easy." An unfamiliar male voice, barely a whisper, sounded directly behind her.

A hand cuffed the side of her head. "She's a—"

"Right. Let's get ready," the leader said.

His voice she recognized. It was burned on her brain. He talked with Connor. He acted as if he knew all about her husband. And now he talked with someone who hid in the shadows behind her. Another man so quiet she hadn't even sensed his presence.

"You have to give Connor more time." She had no idea if that was true but she needed noise. Needed them to talk to her before all of the sensations bombarding her dragged her under.

Then a presence stood right behind her. Not touching but close enough for something in her skin to tingle.

"Don't underestimate him."

It was the voice. The one she didn't recognize. And the fury in those three words had her shivering so hard she couldn't stop.

CONNOR LOWERED THE BINOCULARS. Snipers used them for a reason. This set had increased magnification and brightness so that being more than two hundred yards away from his target didn't matter at all. These worked for up to a thousand yards, so he could easily see two armed men walking around inside the cabin and the top of another person's head. Even in the poor light he could tell the hair color matched Jana's.

That was enough for him. He checked his bulletproof vest and started to leave the protective outcropping of rocks where he hid with Cam. Connor was careful not to make too much noise but rubble and rocks crunched beneath his feet.

Cam grabbed his arm. "Hold up."

That wasn't happening. Already Connor's mind spun with a list of horrible things his wife could have endured. He needed her out of there right now. "Jana doesn't have more time."

"According to the GPS in her phone she's not even in there."

Throughout the entire tense flight across the country, they'd talked strategy. Connor's second-in-command, Davis Weeks, stayed back at Annapolis headquarters and provided intel via the comm they all wore during operations. Even now the entire team listened in and stayed connected via earpieces and watches.

All Davis's tracking and calculations put Jana at the charity headquarters a few miles away. Connor knew that was wrong and Davis agreed. "The GPS is too easy. It's a setup," Connor said.

Cam nodded. "Probably."

"They would have found her cell and planted it somewhere else as a red herring. That's what the guy on the phone was talking about when he dared me to find her."

"Still, we need to be smart."

"Listen to the man." Holt Kingston made the comment in the comm then appeared in front of Connor two seconds later.

Connor blinked, trying to figure out why the entire three-man Corcoran traveling team surrounded him all of a sudden. He'd grabbed Cam and brought him along more because he was in the house when the call came than anything else.

Without Cam, Connor would have called in favors and caught a private flight on his own, only clueing the team in once he was gone. This was about Jana. It was his fight.

Cam clearly hadn't agreed and had, instead, immediately sounded the alarm. Now Holt, the de facto leader of this squad who answered only to Connor, and Shane Baker showed up. They were supposed to be taking some time off after a tense kidnap rescue in Mexico. So much for vacation.

"When did you two get here?" Connor asked.

Shane shrugged. “We booked it over here after Davis and Cam called us in.”

“Which you should have done.” Holt emphasized his point by checking his gun. When he looked up again he was every inch the former special ops soldier—formidable, serious and lethal.

That described the entire team and was doubly true for the traveling members. They spent their lives on the road and seemed to prefer it that way. Corcoran operated as a private security firm. When the training they offered wasn’t followed and things went wrong, Corcoran cleaned up the mess.

Holt was the ultimate expert in planning victim extractions. With Cam, a guy who once worked in black ops so secret even Connor couldn’t find intel on the work, and Shane, Holt’s best friend and former partner in special ops, this was not a group a smart person took on.

Still, this was not just any assignment to Connor. “This is personal.”

Cam exhaled, his frustration clear in the lines on his forehead and tick in his jaw. “Jana is important to all of us.”

Holt talked right on as if he had the go-ahead. “Shane’s done some recon, and you’re right about the charity offices. Looks like a trap. There were four men stationed outside—hiding, but we found them—and no heat signatures inside.”

Shane hissed. “That doesn’t necessarily mean—”

“Don’t.” Connor took a threatening step forward. He knew what Shane was suggesting, that maybe Jana wasn’t alive, but Connor couldn’t hear it. Wouldn’t let it be true.

“How did you find us?” Cam asked, diffusing the tension pulsing around them.

“Your GPS works fine.” Holt looked around. “So why do you think she’s here over any cave in the area?”

Connor handed over the binoculars and pointed to the falling-down shack in the distance. "Davis said that was the nearest usable building."

"Didn't you hear Joel's report?" Cam asked.

Holt shook his head. "The comm blinked out on us for a few minutes. Not sure why."

"Joel repositioned a satellite to provide extra surveillance for us here." Cam clicked a button on his watch and showed the small screen to Holt and Shane. "Joel also somehow broke into the charity office's alarm feed and rewound to see Jana being dragged away there hours ago. A black truck drove in this direction. It looks like the abandoned one we nearly tripped over on our way here."

Connor appreciated Cam filling in the blanks. Even saying the words, thinking about some man grabbing and hurting Jana, made fury thunder in his veins. Since Joel Kidd operated as their tech whiz and managed to get the confirmation, that was good enough for Connor.

Shane grunted. "Gotta love Joel's tech voodoo."

They had to move, but Connor needed to make a few things clear. He had priorities and they were all going to be bound by them. He was the boss and this was nonnegotiable. "Before we start—"

Holt held up a hand. "Connor."

"Don't say it, man." Shane shook his head. "Just don't."

Connor hoped the operation went down smooth and fast, but he knew from experience things could go wrong. Innocents could get caught in the crossfire. "You save her. I don't care what happens to me. You get her out alive and uninjured."

"We all go in and we all come out." Holt's voice rose as he talked.

"Right." Connor didn't test his men further. They got it. Didn't like it, but he knew they understood. He pointed at Shane and Holt. "You two cause a diversion at the front and draw the gunfire away from Jana and the inside of the cabin. Cam and I go in hard through the windows at the back."

Cam nodded. "Done."

"Let's move." Holt said the words then took off with Shane. They ran at a crouch, quiet and fast, blending into the horizon.

Connor and Cam took off in the opposite direction. Scanning the area, Connor watched for reinforcements and more attackers. Only two men with Jana struck him as light. It could mean the guy who wanted him to come to Utah depended on his subterfuge at the charity office working. Or it could mean something else. Either way, Connor was on edge as he kept his mind focused on the task ahead.

Per protocol, the comm stayed quiet as they circled wide to the back of the building. Connor ran to the far side. His back hit the wall and he slid down until he balanced on the balls of his feet. One hand snaked up as he tested the window and found it locked. He knew Cam had the same experience when the word *locked* came over the comm in an almost soundless whisper.

Connor wanted to spring up and look inside, but he waited, doing a mental countdown as he reached for patience and held for the signal. The line clicked once. That meant they were ready to go.

Four against two, and with Corcoran in the mix, Connor knew this should be an easy takedown. Clean and quick. But that depended on it being surprise-free and he'd been around long enough to know things rarely turned out that way.

A second click came right before a loud crash. Men's

voices filled the quiet air. They were yelling, then the bangs started. Gunfire and shuffling. More shouting.

Connor didn't wait another minute. He jumped up and stepped out just far enough to get leverage. Ducking with his shoulder forward and head tucked, he ran. His body slammed into the window and the hit jolted through him. Glass shattered around him, the crackling and crunching filled his ears.

Gunfire continued to pop as momentum had him flying through the air and sliding across the hard floor on his hip. He rolled, keeping as much bare skin away from the sharp and broken edges as possible. When he stopped spinning, he looked up and saw Jana tied to a chair a few feet away. Shards of glass were scattered around her feet and a few caught the light where they stuck in her hair and across her lap.

He took in her wide eyes and the tear rolling down her cheek and scooted over to her, ignoring the crunching underneath him. When the shots grew closer and footsteps pounded on the front porch and near the open door, he gripped his knife and sawed through the bindings on her legs. After a few cuts, her ankle kicked free and she moved on the chair. It wasn't until that moment that Connor noticed the second spray of glass in front of him and Cam crouched down, loosening the ties on her arms.

Just as they released her, the door slammed open. Connor didn't hesitate. He yanked on Jana's arm and tugged her to the floor on top of him. Firing with one hand, he used the other to shield her under him while they flipped over. Glass crushed under his arm and cut into the back of his hand where he cradled her head, keeping it off the dangerous floor.

One man peeked into the doorway then his head shot back out of sight again. The second time the guy's gun came around first. Right when Connor spied one eye, the guy's gun dropped and his body followed face forward to the floor. It took another beat or two for Connor to realize the thunder of gunfire had stopped and silence filled the room.

Blood oozed from the downed man's head and puddled around his hair. Holt and Shane stepped over the lifeless body as they stormed inside.

Seeing his men snapped the stillness that had frozen Connor in place. "Everyone okay?"

"Two down and all is quiet." Holt didn't stop watching Jana as he talked.

Careful not to crush her underneath him, Connor looked down and stared into the big brown eyes he loved so much. Jana's pale face couldn't hide the high cheekbones and sexy mouth that drove him wild. After months apart there was so much he wanted to say. But not in front of an audience.

He went with the obvious. "Are you hurt?"

Without saying a word, she reached up and slipped a hand around the back of his neck. When she tugged his head down, he didn't fight her. Inches separated them until his mouth covered hers and men standing around didn't matter. Everything faded into the background except her and those lips and the kiss that sucked him under just as it always did.

His mouth wandered and his breath caught. He wanted to deepen the kiss. To ask her to come home right there, to forget all that had just happened and not take no for an answer. He settled for what she let him have now and tried to make that enough.

After nuzzling his nose in her hair, he forced his head to lift. "Jana?"

"You came." She shifted and looked around. "And brought the big guns with you."

How could she doubt he would get there? He would have stolen a plane if that's what it took. "Of course."

She still didn't move. Just laid in his arms and let Connor keep the majority of her body off the glass on the floor.

Her gaze went back to him. "Did you get them all?"

"Yes."

It was what she needed to hear and it wasn't a complete lie. They got the ones they saw and the ones shooting back. As soon as he got her off the floor, he'd worry about the other men lurking out there and try to figure out why someone wanted him enough to take Jana. If the person knew him at all, he had to know touching her was a death sentence.

A smile kicked up at the corner of her mouth as she started to sit up with his help. "Funny, but I thought you were going to tell me it was too easy."

He winced. His wife wasn't stupid, so he didn't treat her that way. "Well…"

The corners of her mouth fell. "Connor?"

"It was."

Chapter Three

At Connor's words, Jana shook her head and forced her mind to clear. She looked at the impressive devastation around her. The walls of the small cabin were all torn up from gunfire and glass covered the floor.

The front door hung from its hinges and a wall of muscled, fierce men surrounded her. She knew each of them would protect her. All would step in front of her and take a bullet. That's who they were—quiet men who saved others for a living and refused the title of hero…no matter how much they deserved it.

Seeing Connor hit her like it always did. Made her breathless as her stomach performed a little dance. From the beginning, the combination of broad shoulders, black hair and dark eyes had battered her control.

He carried his emotional baggage with him and it showed in the serious expression on his face. He wasn't pretty. He was tough and sexy and still had the power to make her heart stutter.

But the hesitation followed by the admission felled her. Putting aside the fear buzzing in her head and making her dizzy, she grabbed on to Connor's arm and let him lift her to her feet. Pieces of glass hung from the ends of her hair and stabbed into her legs through her jeans, but she ignored all that.

She wanted to hide in a corner, but she forced her body to remain steady, even as she kept a hand locked around Connor's arm. "How many men did you take out?"

"Two."

That number was way off from what it should have been. She closed her eyes for a second and tried to remember the voices and faces of her attackers and kidnappers. Panic crashed over her but the feel of Connor's hand over hers helped her push through it.

She swallowed hard to regain her voice and composure. "Let me see the bodies."

With a hand skimming her hair, he frowned at her. "You sure?"

The soothing gesture almost did her in. The urge to curl up in his arms and let him make it all better nearly swamped her. She wasn't weak and after a lifetime of being dragged around to camps and medical centers across the most poverty-stricken parts of the world by her doctor father she didn't shake easily. But the knee-buckling kiss she gave Connor the minute the shooting ended was only part of what she wanted from him.

Drawing in a deep breath, she pushed her needs aside. There would be time later. They had so much to talk about and work through. She'd never intended to stay away from home this long but a simple solution to their complex issues still hadn't hit her.

Now all she wanted was these men home and safe and her in bed with Connor over her. Once she survived this, maybe that could happen.

"I should check." She eased up on the clench on Connor's arm. If she let them see the terror still racing through her, they'd go deeper into male protection mode and she needed them to focus on what was happening around them, not on her.

"What?" Holt asked.

She glanced over at one of Connor's team leaders. She'd liked Holt from the beginning. Raised in Hawaii by his Japanese mother, Holt protected his sister and fought for his country. He was rock solid, like all the team members were, but there was something about the way he usually maintained silence that made her smile. He backed up Connor and she knew her husband's life was safe in Holt's hands. Still, Holt wasn't a "yes man" and Connor described that as Holt's best quality.

"To see if these two were there when I got trapped at the charity." Because if they weren't then there were even more men out there ready to hunt Connor down.

He put a hand on each forearm and turned her to face him again. His intense stare bored into her. "What does that mean?"

"Back at the office two came in the front, waving guns around. I ran to the back and there were four more out there. Waiting."

Holt shook his head. "Damn."

He motioned to Shane and each man took an arm of the dead man and dragged him to the porch. They moved fast and kept low. The guy got a quick patdown then she saw a flash. Before any of it registered in her brain they were back inside.

Shane leaned the broken door against the frame and each took a position on the side of the opening and looked into the dark night. He stopped only long enough to hand something off to Cam.

"You're lucky to be alive." The chain continued as Cam pivoted and stepped between Jana and Connor, holding something in his palm.

"They clearly wanted me alive to get to Connor here." She glanced down and noticed Cam held a cell. With a swipe of his thumb, a man's face appeared on the screen. Eyes closed and face bruised. She leaned in closer to get a better look. "What's this?"

"I got a photo of the guy Holt took down outside and sent it to Davis for facial identification." Cam moved the cell around. "This is it."

A shiver ran through her when she recognized the guy as the one who touched her hair. "That's one of them. One that chased me, I mean."

Connor broke his hold on her and tapped a finger against his ear. "Hey, Davis, any luck on the ID check?"

Shane frowned as he touched his ear. "Davis?"

Holt followed suit and did a comm check. When he shook his head, she knew they'd somehow lost contact with the Maryland office. The way Cam and Connor crowded around her only highlighted the potential new danger.

"What happened?" she asked, amazed at how small and quiet her voice sounded.

Connor motioned for Cam to pocket the phone. "Everyone stay on guard. Could be nothing."

The shaking in her bones suggested otherwise. If she shook any more her teeth would rattle. "Or it could be something, like a blocked signal."

She knew just enough to be frozen in fear. There were devices, ways to keep people from communicating on an internal system. Ways to cut people off and make them more vulnerable.

"We're going to assume the signal was momentarily lost." Holt swore when a stray piece of wood from the broken door crunched under his foot. "Okay, let's run through this. There was nothing on the guy outside or the one on the porch. No ID or obvious markings."

She knew he meant tattoos and markings. More than once the team had tangled with some nasty international gang types during kidnap recovery, so the team clearly thought that was a possibility here.

There was no good answer, but trained mob assassins struck her as one of the worst possibilities. She rushed to give the team as full a picture as possible so they could assess. "There were four men here earlier."

Connor froze in the act of typing something into his black watch. "What?"

The news she was about to deliver would get them all moving. It wouldn't go over well but evading was never the answer with this group. "Actually, there were seven men altogether. Six back at the charity office, including the leader, when they took me. Then when I woke up—"

"They knocked you out?"

She nodded because the red wash of anger on Connor's face and mumbled profanity she heard from the others said enough. She didn't need to add to whatever was happening inside of him—or any of them—with more words about that.

"When I got here, I heard another voice," she said. "A guy behind me, so I couldn't see him. He seemed to be calling the shots and the one the leader from the attack on the charity office answered to."

"We still have four hanging around at the charity. Or we did. They could be mobilizing and on the way here by now," Shane said.

Holt nodded but his attention never wavered from whatever he watched outside. "We should assume that."

"There are men over there now?" Panic surged through her all over again. She had protection. She had them.

"Were, but probably still are."

Shane's confirmation was enough for her. She turned back to Connor, made him focus on her over the emotions spinning through him. Touching him was like touching stone. Anger vibrated off of him as he held his body stiff.

She worked to keep the worry out of her voice. "We need to warn Marcel and the others to stay away from the office. I don't want anyone else dragged into this, whatever it is."

"Marcel is…?" Cam asked.

"Marcel Lampari. He runs the charity she's working for." Connor didn't break eye contact with her. "He'll be fine. Go back to the part about the other men who attacked you."

This subject, Marcel, was a sensitive one. She knew Connor blamed Marcel for so much. When she worked overseas years ago and masked gunmen intercepted a vaccine shipment with her on board, Connor and his group got her out. That's how they met. In a mix of adrenaline, heat and terror, which she should have seen as a sign of how their marriage would run.

But they'd put the kidnapping incident behind them long ago and fallen in love. Only one topic remained and bubbled up every so often to wallop them. Back then Connor unloaded on Marcel for his poor security and vulnerable distribution channels. The charity had fixed all those issues since then but Connor's distrust of Marcel never faded.

Connor believed Marcel viewed her as more than a fellow worker. That he would leave his wife if Jana showed any interest. She never picked up on whatever Connor saw in Marcel and the man never made a move, but the attraction was very real in Connor's mind and he didn't try to hide it.

When she'd had to get away she'd wrestled with the idea of coming to Utah, fearing it would hurt Connor even more to have her leave and go to Marcel. But she had nowhere else to turn. She'd lost her father when she was twenty and her mother a decade before that. Her life with Connor had been so insular and her need to get away so desperate that without really thinking it through she ran right to the one man sure to infuriate Connor.

She never meant to betray him. She loved Connor and would never cheat on him, but in her haze she messed up. Only two weeks before, Connor confronted her about Marcel during one of their weekly telephone calls and Connor's anger bubbled over. He told her his patience had expired and started a countdown to come get her. She'd hung up on him and now that decision haunted her.

If they had any chance of making their way back to each other they had to work out the Marcel issue, but now was not the time. "Connor, please."

A charged silence lit up the cabin. Even Holt gave a quick look over his shoulder to see what was happening in the center of the room.

Connor finally broke the quiet but did nothing to hide the fury shading his voice. "Cam will warn everyone."

Him not blowing up qualified as a small victory because this topic changed his otherwise steady personality white hot. She took that as a positive sign.

With one last glance at the photos on the cell, the pieces came together in her head. "Not that long before you guys crashed in, there were four people here with me. These two plus the one you talked with on the phone and another."

"How did two get away without any of us seeing them?" Cam asked.

Connor continued to stare at her as he took Cam's cell out of her hands. "Good question, but we're talking about people with skills. These aren't petty thieves. These guys look like professionals and the guy on the phone specifically asked for me."

Shane blew out a long breath. "The news just keeps getting better."

Her heart hammered and the thumping of the beat in her ears had her inhaling in an effort to calm down. She didn't know what would happen next or how they would get out of the cabin, so she said one of the things she absolutely needed to share. "Thank you all for coming."

"There wasn't a chance we wouldn't." Cam reached over and squeezed her hand. "And not just us. We had to keep the Maryland team from heading out here, too."

"You're one of us." Shane treated her to a wink before looking away again.

Connor moved into her line of sight. "Yes, you are."

Some of the anxiety pinging around inside of her faded. "Connor, I need you to know—"

He put a finger over her lips. "We have a lot to talk about, and we will because I am done living like this, but all of that has to wait until you're safe."

She wanted to spill it all. Tell him how much she still loved him and spell out all of their problems and make him talk through each one with her.

Forget about the presence of his men and the danger. If this was it, if this was how it ended, she wanted him to know she had never stopped loving him and never would. He was hers forever.

But the closed look on his face and slight shake of his head told her this was not the time. Certainly not the place. "Okay."

He touched her cheek. "Did you recognize the voice or face of the man who talked to me on the phone?"

"No." And she had tried. She'd turned over every memory and all the bits Connor shared of his life before her.

"Folks." Holt cleared his throat. "We're going to have sunrise soon and we have some people to warn."

"Right" Connor rubbed his hands together. "We need to get word out to your coworkers."

She knew that cost him something and rested her forehead against his chin to let him know how much it meant. "Thank you."

A strange red light flashed through the room. She spied a dot and watched it streak along the wall. Connor followed her gaze before his grip tightened.

"Get down!" he yelled as he knocked the chair over and dragged her to the floor with it.

She blinked and he had her on her stomach, wedged under his body with her head against the upturned chair's wooden seat. The first boom had her lifting up in shock. Before she could say anything or even think, Connor put a hand on her head and pushed her down again.

She could see from their black shoes that Holt and Shane moved around. She heard shuffling off to the side and assumed Cam kept shifting and firing.

"Do not move." Connor spoke right into her ear. He could have been yelling, but with all the noise crashing and thumping it barely registered as a whisper.

Then the weight against her back lifted. Turning, she watched him sprint toward the broken window he came through earlier. As he got there a bullet clipped the frame and wood splintered right by his face. He ducked but not before a piece clipped his cheek.

She bit back a scream as wood kicked up around her. She sat up and her shoes slipped against the floor as she skidded on her butt, looking for any square foot of the floor not covered by debris.

"Incoming." Red lights raced over Cam and he ducked. "Jana, tuck in a ball."

She shook her head as she watched Cam's mouth move and heard his voice, but the words wouldn't register. She was about to warn him about the lights when Connor's body slammed into her. He skidded across the floor almost hitting the far wall. Glass crunched all around her as they slid.

One second he stood a few feet away. The next, he covered her, pressing her down as his body jerked and he grunted in her ear.

As fast as it started, the gunfire broke off again. She peeked over Connor's shoulder and saw the front door had fallen over and both Holt and Shane were gone. Pieces of wood and shards from the wall and chair littered the floor.

Cam crouched next to her head. "Are you okay?"

She looked up, thinking to reassure him. But his entire focus stayed on Connor.

"What's going on?" She tried to shift but the weight on her grew heavier and she only made it to her side. The pieces fell together as panic roared through her. "Connor?"

Cam put a hand on her shoulder. "Hold still a second."

She grabbed at Cam's hand, clawing in panic from the narrow-eyed concern on his face. "Is he hurt?"

Footsteps thumped on the hard floor as Holt stepped back inside. "We have four down… What's going on?"

"Help me." Worry edged Cam's voice as he caught her hand in his.

Holt dropped to his knees on her other side. "What are you doing?"

"It's Connor." Cam cleared his throat. "We need this vest off so I can take a look."

They wore matching flatlined expressions that had her heartbeat nosediving. She flipped over and moved, trying to get a better look at what was happening behind her.

She shoved at Connor's shoulder. "Answer me."

He swore as he rolled onto his side on the floor next to her. "I'm fine."

He shifted up to his elbow, but Holt pushed him down on his stomach and held him there with a strong hand.

The sound of Velcro ripped through the otherwise quiet room as Cam stepped over her and dug his hands underneath Connor's body.

"You were shot in the back?" The words stuck in her throat as she struggled to breathe.

Cam carefully peeled the vest off and exhaled as he fell back on his butt. "We're good."

"Are you sure?" She struggled to sit up and look over the two broad backs in her way. She scanned Connor's sweat-soaked T-shirt and the good news sunk in. "There's no blood."

Cam nodded. "The bullet went into the vest."

"It held. Always nice when the equipment works." Holt cuffed Connor on the shoulder then stood up.

Her legs refused to move. Relief hit her hard enough to send her slumping against the floor. "I can't believe you were shot."

One of Cam's eyebrows lifted. "It was either him or you."

The scene replayed in her mind. Her on the floor. Cam calling out a warning. The bright flash of red light she only now remembered. It cut through the air and then Connor smacked into her. That meant one thing.... He'd risked his life to save her.

If anything had been off, even by a fraction, he'd be dead. The air whooshed right back out of her lungs. "You could have miscalculated and been hit."

Connor sat up, wincing as he moved. "I didn't." The room started spinning and a wave of dizziness set in.

"Are you hurt?"

"I bet he's sore as hell." Holt snorted. "When the bullet slams into you it hurts like a—"

A sharp look from Connor stopped whatever else Holt

might have said. Stretching and rubbing his back, Connor stood up. "What do we have outside?"

That one made Holt smile. "A bunch of dead shooters."

Connor reached down and helped her to her feet. She hung on just in case her knees gave out on her, which, with the crushing despair at the thought of Connor being shot still zipping through her head, was a distinct possibility. "You got them all?"

Holt shrugged. "The ones that didn't run away."

Of course they got the bad guys. That's how the Corcoran Team operated. They protected and they won. She'd come to depend on that so much that she couldn't conceive of any of them getting injured. It's probably what kept her from living every hour in fear.

Davis and Holt followed Connor's example and led without even trying. Pax, Davis's brother, and Joel provided some of the team's lighter moments back in Maryland but were deadly lethal when necessary.

She knew all of them except Ben. From her conversations with Connor about the battles Ben had taken on during his former job with NCIS, she had no doubt he fit in fine with the rest of them.

"I took photos of…" Shane stopped just inside the doorway. His gaze bounced around the cabin-turned-shooting-gallery. "What did I miss?"

"Nothing." Connor tugged her closer and put a hand just below her belt.

No way was she forgetting what just happened. "Let me see your back."

His hold didn't lessen. "It's fine."

"Okay, well, I have more photos." Shane glanced at Holt and a look passed between them before Shane handed the camera to Connor.

Jana couldn't read the guys' expressions but knew they

engaged in some sort of silent conversation. She guessed she was the subject. Her or Connor, or both.

Connor started to hand the cell over then stopped. "I hate to ask—"

"I'll look." She took it before he could analyze and start frowning. "Huh. Well, I have bad news."

"More?" Cam asked, the amusement evident in his voice.

Connor's stern expression didn't slip. "What?"

"I only recognize this one." She pointed at the second photo. She scrolled the images back and forth. "These three were not part of the crowd when I got kidnapped."

"So there are even more of them. Great." Shane swore under his breath. "And for the record, I hate that you're now an assignment."

"She's not." Connor leaned into her and his breath caressed her cheek. "Which one was the leader?"

She loved the closeness but knew her answer would put him straight back into work-concentration mode. "None. The leader, the one who called you, isn't here. He got away."

"Which means?" Cam asked.

Connor's shoulders stiffened as he stood up straight again. "We still have a problem."

In her mind, that qualified as a huge understatement.

Chapter Four

Luc Pearson gathered his group under a towering rock pile near the charity offices. The storm had passed over, taking the kicking winds with it. Now the sky brightened as they edged closer to daybreak. That meant time was running out.

Even though the area had emptied out during the night, Luc wanted this part of the game wrapped up before people woke and started buzzing around. The last thing he needed was more witnesses. There had been enough death.

Which brought his mind back to the group. He looked around the semicircle of his remaining men. The Corcoran team had knocked out six trained shooters without breaking a sweat. He'd been warned about the team's skills but this amount of loss wasn't part of the deal.

Rich Stapleton shifted his weight from foot to foot. "You said there would be one, maybe two of them. We're looking at a full team with a lot of firepower and impressive training."

"We still have the advantage." Bruce Harding's flat tone rang out in the still night. "This isn't their turf."

Rich scoffed. "You think we're winning this thing? I have a bunch of dead bodies that suggest otherwise. Bodies of good men who were told this would be a quick stint."

Luc decided not to point out the obvious, about how

those so-called experts died without putting up much of a fight. Truth was, the lopsided battle surprised him. He'd studied the files of all the hires for this job. All but Bruce. He was the boss's pick and he acted as if he was untouchable. Probably because he was.

But Rich and his crew operated on another level. They didn't have the boss's protection or his trust. If he wanted them gone, they'd be terminated and that meant quieted so they couldn't talk. Bruce had made it clear that was one of his duties. If the word came down, he'd handle it.

Luc had found Rich through contacts. Locating the right guy, one who walked away from the army edgy and frustrated, blaming the government for his failings, proved easy enough. With all the options out there, Luc had insisted on former military and disillusioned.

Turned out Rich knew plenty of the well-trained-but-done-with-rules and the so-called bright-lines-between-right-and-wrong types. Men whose loyalties could be bought. Rich had served with some of them and knew others by reputation.

Luc culled through potential additions to the group with Rich, framing just the right collection of men who had few ties to each other and a deep need for cash. Rich picked the squad but Luc had final approval. And now many of them were gone.

"Apparently Connor Bowen travels with reinforcements." Bruce tapped the blade of his knife against his open palm but never lifted his head.

"Would have been nice to know that instead of being told he'd rush out here and make himself an easy target."

One of the men offered the insight. Luc didn't remember the guy's name and didn't intend to learn it. He preferred think about the men in terms of where they lived. That made this one Reno.

"How did they get the woman without any bloodshed on their side?" Rich asked.

That one was easy. Luc had explained the failure to his boss earlier and repeated it now. "Your buddies failed."

Reno took a threatening step forward. "Watch it."

Rich signaled Reno and another man to stay back. "Tread carefully."

Luc watched a pickup truck ride the dirt road a few hundred yards away. When it turned and headed toward the town, or what qualified as one out here, he let out the breath he was holding. "Why? It's not as if these guys can hit a target."

"Why don't I show you how skilled I am?" Reno asked.

"You think this is funny, Luc? That standing there relaying the boss's orders means you're safe from us?" Rich managed to squint and telegraph menace at the same time.

Luc's hand slid to the gun slipped into his belt. He'd paid for their time but these guys weren't exactly known for deep and abiding loyalty. "I think I paid for competence and I'm not getting it."

"But we don't work for you, now do we?" Rich's men grunted in agreement with Rich's comment. "Funny how you forgot to mention you were only the middleman—powerless—when you hired us."

They didn't have time for insubordination and Luc's tolerance had hit its end. "You get paid from me, so I am your boss."

"Nah, I don't think so." Rich shook his head. "Who else is working this?"

Luc's hand inched closer to the gun.

Bruce beat him to it. "That's enough."

He morphed from bored and disinterested to battle mode in two seconds. He didn't lift a weapon or even move a step. The grave delivery and sharp whack of his voice did it.

Luc had served with men like Bruce. They demanded attention and when they didn't get it, they unleashed a wrath that destroyed everything. Luc suspected Bruce hovered about an inch away from snapping now.

No matter how clear the message, Rich appeared to ignore it. He hitched his chin in Bruce's general direction. "Why should I listen to you?"

Reno nodded. "Good question."

And there it was. Luc stepped out of the way just in time. The words had barely left Rich's mouth when Bruce stepped right into Rich's face with a hand wrapped around the back of his neck. With his other hand he pressed a knife against Rich's throat. "Want to ask again?"

Rich thrashed until the knife pricked skin, then he went still. "What are you—"

"Do not move unless you want a deeper cut." Bruce grabbed Rich's bulletproof vest in his fist and dragged it right up to his throat, nearly chocking him. "Tell your friends to step back before I slice you."

Rich didn't hesitate. Didn't move, either. "Listen to him."

"Good." Bruce leaned in even closer to his prey. "Now I have one word for you."

"What?"

Luc had to give Rich credit. His voice stayed steady and he didn't beg. He used his free hand to wave his men back and Luc guessed that one gesture saved a bloodbath.

"Deniability." Bruce emphasized all six syllables. "We don't want details. Details put you in danger. Makes you usable to guys like Connor and a liability to us. The kind of liability a sharpshooter might eliminate with a shot to the forehead."

When Bruce shoved him away, Rich stumbled back. He

came to a halt and tugged on the bottom of his vest. "You made your point."

"Good."

For one more beat, Rich held Bruce's stare then turned to Luc. "So what now? We have them trapped in a shack. I say we blow it up."

Tempting, but not the plan. If he had his choice, Luc would take that tactic and cut his losses. But his boss was a very angry man with a definite plan. A powerful man bent on revenge. "We need them to escape. To believe they got away and turn sloppy."

Rich snorted. "Why?"

"The plan hasn't changed." Bruce jumped in before Luc could answer. "We want Connor and his wife on the run. The others are expendable and it's time for them to go."

The other men mumbled but Rich put the feelings into words. "You think this Connor is a guy you can mess with? Track down like an animal? No way."

But Luc understood this part. He had a wife once. Lost her in an instant at the hands of a drunk driver. He knew what he would do to bring her back. What lengths he would have employed to protect her if he could only go back in time, including taking the killing blow for her. Worse, he was intimately familiar with how a man pushed to the edge was capable of anything.

"When he's out on his own, without backup and trying to keep his wife alive, he'll fold. If we have her we can make him do anything. Racing across the country was just the start." Luc spoke with absolute certainty.

He didn't have to guess or wonder. He didn't even need to hear it from his boss. The fear in Connor Bowen's voice over the phone said it all—his wife came first.

Rich didn't look convinced. Even in the limited light, the frown lines and twist of his mouth were clear. "He didn't strike me as the collapsing type. It's more likely he'll double down and become a killing machine."

The grating sound of Bruce's knife sliding into a metal sheath stopped conversation and drew all of their attention. "Let's get back to the team and discuss what we do to get rid of them this time around. I don't know about you, but I'm sick of losing men."

"And we can't afford to be down many more." Last thing Luc could do was call in reinforcements. This job had a ticking clock and the countdown had started. "So we separate and destroy."

If possible, Rich's frown deepened even further. "Meaning?"

"I think explosion does have a nice ring to it." Luc had the supplies piled in the back of his nondescript truck, just waiting to light up the sky before morning dawned. Nothing would trace back to him, not even the truck he bought for cash under a fake name.

Bruce's dark chuckle echoed around them. "I like the finality of your suggestion."

They could think whatever they wanted so long as they got the job done…this time. Luc scanned the dwindling group. "You have one assignment."

Something in his tone had even Bruce looking around. "Which is?"

"Connor stays, but don't let the other team members get out alive." It was the one sure way to knock the man off his game. Take out his friends and leave him reeling.

And to save his own hide, that is exactly what Luc promised his boss only a few minutes ago he would do… and he'd deliver.

HOLT LOWERED HIS FIST and gave the all-clear signal. The group started walking again under the blanket of stars.

Whatever he heard out among the red rocks and tree stubs must have turned out to be innocent. Possibly an animal and clearly nothing with a weapon. With his tracking skills, he'd know. Which was why Connor put Holt in the lead.

After a brief argument where Connor insisted Jana wear his bulletproof vest, they'd slipped out of the shack one at a time, with Shane and Holt in front drawing attention away from Jana. Connor doubted she even understood the tactic. Reality was, with the lineup then and gathering of his men around her now they'd have ample warning if someone went after her. They'd all sacrifice their lives for her.

Their willingness to die for her, for them, mattered to Connor. He didn't take that sort of devotion for granted. He appreciated all of his men and grew more grateful every day for their agreement to throw in with him. People depended upon their skills and he'd come to expect them to stay honed and ready.

They ran drills because he insisted, but he knew they'd keep in shape and sharp without any prodding from him. That's who they were—solid and stable. The very best at their jobs.

Connor checked the comm again. "Davis?"

"I just tried." Shane shook his head. "Got nothing."

Pebbles crunched and their feet fell in a steady cadence. When they broke through a mass of trees and over the rise of loose rock, Holt motioned for them to crouch down.

Up until then Jana had stayed quiet and marched along beside Connor. She had his belt in a loose hold between two fingers. If he walked too fast, she'd tug and he'd slow down. They'd rehearsed the system and used it the last time someone grabbed her.

Back then they didn't know each other and he'd had to run through the silent signal and convince her not to talk during their escape. This time she knew making noise could get them all killed, and didn't question.

Squatting on the balls of her feet, she leaned into his shoulder and whispered against his cheek. "What's happening?"

Every muscle pulled tight from the adrenaline rushing through him. He wanted to sprint to the car and lock her in a seatbelt and send her away. Beating that instinct back took most of his energy, but he still wanted to touch her.

With a hand on her lower back, Connor pointed to the clearing ahead and the dark jeeps that blended into the skyline. "That's our ride."

Holt took a final look around then nodded. "We're clear."

"Wait." Jana caught Connor's arm as he started to rise. "Those men could be anywhere."

Connor understood the fear and doubt. She'd been manhandled—something he still couldn't think about without being swamped by homicidal rage—and threatened. She'd survived a hail of bullets and him tackling her. He couldn't exactly fault her for expecting danger to lurk under every rock.

But they couldn't sit still. Waiting made them easy to locate and even easier to hit. "We've got two cars. Shane and Holt are going to head out and warn Lampari and the other office workers you gave the contact information for, as promised."

Connor breezed over the other man's name. Dead wife or not, Connor didn't buy Marcel's story. More than once over the years Connor had caught the man staring at Jana. They'd get together for events or during those times when Jana picked up some of the charity's work to ease Marcel's load. His gaze would linger when it landed on Jana and his smile would brighten.

No way did that guy view Jana as a daughter or whatever ridiculous thing she thought. Connor knew how a man looked at a woman he wanted to take to bed, and he saw that need in Marcel. Saw and wanted to pound it right out of the guy.

Jealousy didn't sit well with Connor. Up until a few months ago Jana didn't try to inflame it. She brushed off his concerns about her dear old boss while insisting she felt nothing but admiration for him. But when she wanted space and needed time away, Marcel threw his arms wide open and she ran into them. That act ate away at Connor. Burned right through him.

He forced his mind to put it aside. To compartmentalize. He'd sweep her to safety and then they'd talk. Later when the danger cleared and he knew she couldn't be dragged into whatever mess from his life sucked her under this time, he'd unload and demand she do the same.

Time had passed and his anger switched from intense and fiery to a slow burn. He had a front-row seat to Davis putting aside his fears and starting a life with the woman he'd always loved. They had a baby on the way. Talk about walking into danger.

Davis worried and planned and ruthlessly separated his home life from his work life. His brother Pax talked about proposing to his girlfriend, and Joel and Ben were both on the road to forever with their significant others.

They'd all figured out a way to marry the danger of the job with the life they wanted. Connor once thought he had, too, but it had slipped away from him and he wanted it back. He'd grab it no matter how much of his dignity he had to sacrifice to do it.

But he had to get her out of this situation alive first. That meant delivering the news sure to raise her defenses. "You're going with Cam."

"Where?" One word loaded with frustration and accompanied by a rush of red to her cheeks bright enough for him to see in the semidarkness.

"What are you doing in this scenario?" Holt asked.

Grateful for the reprieve, Connor went with Holt's question over Jana's. "Heading to the charity office and seeing what we have there."

Cam shot Connor the side eye. "You want backup?"

The conversation kept rolling along but Jana didn't. She stopped right in the middle of the open. Stood still as if daring him to a debate. "Where am I going with Cam?"

"You need to keep moving." Connor reached for her but she shrugged away.

She wasn't stupid. She knew this was the kind of stand he would hate. The way Holt scanned the horizon and grumbled under his breath, he didn't care for it, either.

Not that the joint foul mood affected her. She crossed her arms and stared Connor down. "Explain what happens after we get into the cars."

"There's a private plane at a small regional airport nearby." Connor had memorized the schematics and had numerous alternate plans. All of them involved getting her back to Maryland and into a secure building. "You and Cam will get on and figure out how to get word to Davis."

"Without being able to contact us, he could already be on the way here," Cam pointed out.

A reasonable thought but not one Connor entertained for even a second. "Not possible."

Holt glanced over his shoulder, finding Connor. "You warned him away?"

"I told him this could all be a scam to attack the office in Annapolis. Lure me out and then go after the house." The place they all worked but where he and Jana lived.

Davis agreed with the worries. Even if he hadn't, Connor would have made his second-in-command promise not to send another team out to Utah.

The man had a child on the way. Even more basic than that, Connor had imposed strict rules about the entire team being together. It couldn't happen. Ever. They split up jobs to eliminate the risk of losing everyone in one horrible moment.

"In other words, we're on lockdown protocol." Shane's voice carried on the quiet night.

"They are all at headquarters—Ben, Joel, Davis and Pax, along with the women. No one leaves. They shoot first." Connor knew he could depend on Davis to carry out those orders. "And no matter what, they do not follow me out here."

"Smart, but not that helpful right now."

"I'm not leaving without you." Jana talked right over Cam. Her voice stayed soft but the underlying thread of steel was tough to miss as she faced Connor.

He'd seen the argument coming. It took Jana a long time to get there, but she eventually did. "This is non-negotiable."

She nodded. "Exactly."

He glanced around at the rapt audience. They all stared at Connor as if waiting to see how he'd wiggle out of this one. In between watching the area, Connor spied the amused expressions. He knew they'd ride him for months about this.

"I need a second with my wife." Connor emphasized the word more for her benefit than theirs.

"Okay." Shane clapped his hands and pointed in the distance. "We'll check the cars and look for tracks."

Connor barely listened. All his concentration centered on his wife. The woman with the lifted chin and fire in her eyes in front of him.

Holt still stood there. "But we need to move soon."

"Yeah. I got it, Holt."

Connor realized something in his tone must have worked because the men turned away and scattered. They went from watching, with their gazes switching from him to her, to taking off.

Connor opened his mouth but her words stopped him. "No, Connor. Don't even try."

"Fine. Get in the car." He refused to argue about this. Not when the answer seemed so obvious.

"Someone is after me, not you."

Since she seemed determined to fight, he complied. "They kidnapped you to get to me, which I would point out has always been my fear. That's the reason behind the drills and weapons lessons. That's why I ran the background check on the woman you met in exercise class."

It all seemed reasonable to him. They needed to be cautious. The more the news of the team's work spread, the more wary he became. There were corporations and countries who wanted Corcoran out of business. That put a target on her back and kept him on edge.

He was about to explain that when she did that woman thing. Made a clicking sound with her tongue as she rolled her eyes. He'd seen the display before and wasn't a fan of either move.

"Don't use this situation as an excuse for your paranoia." Her voice dropped from chilly to ice cold.

Paranoia? "What is that supposed to mean?"

She waved him off and tried to pivot around him. "Nothing."

He stepped into her path, blocking whatever hasty exit she had planned. It wasn't as if she had a lot of options for getting out of here. There wasn't a road or building for miles. Just acres of tumbled rocks and red sand.

In the category of bad ideas—getting into their personal issues in the middle of nowhere, with gunmen lurking in the darkness somewhere—this was a real contender. "I'm not going to fight with you."

"Of course not." She didn't snort but the sarcasm in her voice sounded like she wanted to.

She lost him again. "Meaning?"

"Why would you bother?"

The conversation slid downhill as their voices rose. He didn't even know what they were talking about. "Maybe we could take a second and cool off."

"Fine." She tucked her hands in the front pockets of her pants and rocked back on her heels. "But I think you just proved my point."

"Are you kidding me with this? You are my number one priority." There is no way she could think anything else. "Keeping you safe is all I care about."

"Exactly."

Frustration washed over him until he thought he'd drown in it. He threw up his hands because he had no idea what else to say or do. "What are you saying, or trying not to say, while you make me work for it?"

"I want a marriage, not a jailor."

He stepped in close and ducked his head until they met straight on, face-to-face. "Any chance you'll soon stop talking in cryptic sentences?"

She blew out a long, exaggerated breath. "Why do you think I left?"

He refused to let his mind wander there. He wanted to believe the decision centered on her being restless, not that she needed space. Not that Marcel offered her something or promised anything.

Truth was, Connor had no idea. They talked daily for the first few weeks. She'd insisted she needed time and that she'd be back, but then the weeks passed into months and the call frequency dipped.

The last few talks ended in fighting because he couldn't let the Marcel piece go. Connor hated that guy and all he represented—someone with similar interests to hers, who fought beside her once years ago to help people, who didn't institute precautions designed to protect her but which ticked her off.

Being away from her had ripped him apart. He lied to his team at first, not wanting them to know he'd failed and lost her. Then he stopped offering any excuse and they stopped asking about her.

Only Cam knew Connor had planned to come out and get her. He'd had it set up until Joel got lost on a job in the middle of nowhere West Virginia and took Cam along with him. That delayed everything another few weeks, but Connor was here now. He could say anything.

He went with the soft version of the pain knocking through him. "I think you walked away from me because you wanted something else."

Her eyes softened and her hand swept over his cheek. "I want you. Only you. That has never changed."

"As evidenced by the way you traveled thousands of miles away from me and hunkered down for months." Connor refused to say it. He wouldn't mention the one name sure to wipe that loving look off her face. He wouldn't… "With Marcel."

As predicted, her arm dropped back to her side. "This isn't about him. This is about us and the importance you place on our marriage."

A darkness filled his head and flooded everything. It had his vision cutting in and out. "How can you be the only person on this earth who doesn't see that you are the most important thing in my life? The team gets it, but you refuse to see it."

"Connor, look—"

"You are my life." Her mouth opened then closed again. He decided right there he couldn't take whatever she planned to say. If she wanted to walk away, or be with Marcel or anyone else, Connor couldn't hear it right now. "We'll fight about this later. Right now we need to get to the cars."

They made it one step before Connor heard the clicking. It was faint and unexpected and didn't fit any weapon he recognized. But it was enough to get him moving. He had a hand wrapped around her arm and started tugging her toward the protective cover of the closest boulder when a chilling boom sent flames rocketing into the sky.

The ground shook and the banging didn't stop. The rumbling stole his balance and his feet left the ground. A rush of heated wind punched into him and threw him backward.

One minute he held her and the next she was ripped from his grasp. The air caught them and when he landed the world went dark for a second.

He forced his way through the fatigue dragging him down. His head lolled and his back ached. It took him another second to realize he'd been blown off his feet.

Opening his eyes, he stared up into the scattering of stars above him. Then he saw smoke curling up into the sky. Smelled it.

He pushed up onto his elbows and watched orange flames lick and devour the jeeps. The picture registered and then his mind zoomed to his team. They were there. He had sent them into the fiery explosion.

"No!" The anguished cry tore out of his dry throat.

He made it to his knees before arms clamped around

him from behind. He struggled until Jana's voice rose above the roar of the flames.

"You can't save them," she said in a haunted whisper.

He tried to shrug her off but his arms weighed so much. Pain pummeled him, pounding in his temples and washing over him with each breath. He had to get up. To try to get them out, but nothing made sense. This couldn't be happening.

His hip throbbed. Suddenly he heard a steady buzzing. Shaking his head, he tried to clear out the confusion rolling over him. "What is that?"

She froze behind him. "What?"

Then it hit him. "The phone."

Fumbling and shifting, he grabbed the cell from his pocket. The message from Cam had him blinking.

We're free. Run.

The words clicked and Connor's brain rebooted. He struggled to his feet and lifted her up beside him. Smoke filled the air and somewhere the bomber waited. But they had a chance.

She ran a hand over his hair as tears filled her eyes. "I'm so sorry."

"They're alive."

Her head pulled back as she stared up at him. "Are you sure?"

He'd explain later, celebrate later. Right now they still had killers on their tail who were closing in fast. "We have to move."

Chapter Five

They walked for what felt like miles at a fast clip. Connor had wanted them moving and out of the blaring heat of the sun before the morning hit. He called out orders, or that's how it sounded in Jana's head. She tried to chalk his mood up to the whiplash of desolation from the explosion and relief from the call after. He didn't say it, but she knew he hated being separated from his men.

She also knew her frayed nerves and the dragging exhaustion played tricks on her mind. Every step in the sifting red sand and over the smooth rocks sapped her strength. The heat didn't help.

They escaped the worst. That came with summer, but the intensity and clear sky didn't provide much of a buffer. Neither did her dirty and torn clothes.

She walked all over Annapolis, despite Connor's grumbling, and spent time on a treadmill in the makeshift gym at the house. But after hours of terror and confusion in Utah, her body failed her. She leaned against the cool stone to keep from falling down.

Grimy and sweaty, she wanted a hot shower and a bed and days of sleep. Instead she got a gravel floor and a shaded area about ten feet square where rock walls opened into a sort of cave.

She watched him pace around the entrance to their

temporary hiding place. He stared at his cell's screen as he traveled back and forth over a space little more than a few feet long. "Do you have a signal?"

He didn't raise his head. "No."

"No phone and no GPS."

"Basically."

The guy could argue and lecture for hours on end but he picked now to switch to monosyllabic responses. Lucky her. "Can you do anything with your watch?"

His shoes skidded on the loose rocks as he stopped and glanced over at her. "Like what?"

"I don't know." Her comment seemed silly when he looked at her like that, with the corner of his mouth curled up and his eyes sparkling with mischief, but she'd seen these guys do unbelievable things. Give them a paper clip and a piece of gum and they could rewire a house alarm. It was downright spooky.

"Okay."

He seemed far too amused for her liking. She thought about telling him to knock it off but when she turned her head the world went wavy. With a hand against the smooth edge of the stone she regained her balance.

When she saw his eyes narrow in concern, she blurted out the first thing to pop into her head. "It's just that they seem to perform magic sometimes."

"You should sit down."

"Because I'm babbling?" She looked over her shoulder to the rocks piled up on the side of one wall. With the stark interior and low illumination, the space resembled a jail cell.

"The bobbing and weaving has me more concerned." He put a hand on her elbow.

She leaned into him. "I was trying to get your attention."

He didn't smile at her joke. "Well, you have it."

"So that's what it took."

His fingers tightened against her skin. "Excuse me?"

"Nothing." If she were a different type of woman she might fall down more often. Anything to get him to show a reaction. But games didn't appeal to her. She wanted a marriage, not a constant battle for control.

"You've been up all night and attacked. You deserve some rest." He pocketed the cell and guided her farther into the cave. "Much longer going like this and you could fall over."

"You've had the same long night, plus a flight." Yet he bounced back without as much as a dark circle under his eyes.

He wore the same clothes and they managed to look clean. Except for the scuff of dirt on his black shoes, he could walk into any restaurant and not turn a head…except for the female ones attracted to the tall, dark and oh-so-tempting type.

The whole put-together thing was not new. Connor fit into any situation, could slide in unnoticed or command a room. She had sensed his power the first night she met him. He issued orders and older, bigger and gruffer-looking men jumped to obey.

"No one knocked me out and dragged me from my desk." He smoothed the back of his fingers down her cheek. "The whole tied-up-and-kidnapped thing? That was you, and no matter how much I try I can't forget it."

"You were shot," she said, pointing out the obvious and trying to drag the conversation away from the attack and his guilt. They didn't need additional reminders. Not now when she needed his mind clear, and focus off what happened to her.

"That's a different thing."

She had to smile at that. "Only you would think so."

He demanded so much of himself. The way he pushed his body and mind stunned her. Truth was, she'd always been a little in awe of his self-control. At the beginning that strength, tethered and formidable, excited her. In the past year it suffocated her.

She knew from experience he'd turn her kidnapping over in his mind, analyze it and dissect it. He'd take on the blame and then double down on his security measures.

That's how he operated. He closed her out to protect her, or that's what he claimed. She could never make him understand she craved the closeness he refused to give her.

She sat down on the hard rock and shifted until she found a half-comfortable position. She guessed her butt would either grow sore or go numb in the next few minutes.

He stood over her, hovering, with his feet apart and his hands on his hips. The gun strapped to his side was within easy reach and she knew he had other weapons within a hand's distance. People hunted them down, the world kept exploding and he acted like they were out on a normal hike.

"How can you be so calm?" She folded her hands on her lap to keep from rubbing them together or fidgeting.

"Practice."

Another one-word answer. Clipped but not all that clear. "Are you making a joke?"

He exhaled in that put-upon male tone he did so well. "I'm pointing out that I trained for years to handle stress and danger."

"Your undercover work." She knew all about it, or as much as he could safely say.

"Yes, and now for Corcoran."

He worked for years in what she picked up was a CIA splinter group. He did things that shaped him. Talked about how he went from a military family with a sense of honor and commitment to a black ops expert who grew weary of the game. After he rescued her, he got out. It took months and he hid the long, difficult disconnect from her. Even now she didn't know what he'd promised or sacrificed to start a normal life with her.

Maybe that's where it started. With all the secrets. With him trying so hard to break away from his past.

"You never talk about it." The weight of all those years piled up. She kept trying to lift it off him and open the space between them, but he fought her. Not verbally and certainly not physically, but definitely emotionally.

Even now he made a noise between an exhale and a groan as he took the seat next to her. "Talk about what exactly?"

"The years before you met me."

He rested his elbows on his knees and let his hands hang down between his legs. One thumb rubbed along the calloused palm of his other hand. "They don't matter."

The temptation to reach out and skim her fingers down his back kicked strong. The months apart had taken a toll on her. She missed holding him, making love with him. The simple things like cooking breakfast together and laughing over a movie.

Sitting close, smelling his familiar scent, brought it all rushing back in a punch of longing so powerful she almost doubled over from the force of it. But she forced her mind to hold on to the conversation and her voice to remain steady. "Because?"

He peeked over at her. "I didn't have you."

This man could bring her to her knees. "You were furious with me an hour ago, making claims about Marcel and fighting everything I said and now you're being all sweet. A woman could get confused."

He chuckled. "I know."

"What changed?"

He reached over and slipped a hand over hers. "Almost getting blown up has a way of shifting a man's priorities."

His fingers entwined with hers, sending heat pulsing through her. She didn't realize she was shaking until that moment. "Do you have any idea why someone wants your attention?"

"And grabbed you to get it?" He rubbed his thumb the back of her hand. "It could be anything. I've worked on a lot of cases. Made many enemies."

Rather than battle him about the kidnapping and how he could not have predicted it or prevented it from his office in Maryland, she let it drop. He was determined to take on the blame for what happened to her and no amount of arguing would change his mind. And they needed all of their energy to reason this through.

She cradled his hand in both of hers. "But why now? Did something happen with a case back home?"

"No."

"So you guys have all just been sitting around the family room staring at each other? Drinking beer and watching football?"

"Hardly."

Part of her knew that. Up until recently he used a portion of their telephone calls to talk about the team. He filled her in on Ben and the change in Davis since his marriage. Connor walked her through cases, skipping over details but letting her know what they were all working on.

Being included, even to that small extent, made her ache for home. He kept so much to himself, but he never hid the operations from her. He included her in the conversations. Letting her leave the house without an armed guard was a different thing.

"I'm not hedging." Connor frowned at her. "Nothing out of the ordinary."

As if this man or anyone on the team understood the concept of normal. "What does that mean?"

"I don't know, Jana." He dropped her hand and stood up again. "The usual stuff. Chasing bad guys, ducking gunfire, racing against time."

She almost laughed. She went with slumping her shoulders and letting some of the tension run out of her instead. "That list sounds crazy."

"I know." He braced a palm against the edge of the rock entrance. He traced a pattern in the dirt with the toe of his shoe. "Laying it out sounds cloak-and-dagger, maybe a bit too Hollywood."

"You hate that."

"But the danger is very real. That's part of why I don't discuss the details or do anything that would have you wading into danger." He scoffed. "I guess I failed there since you were tied to a chair a few hours ago."

"No, it's not."

His head shot up and he faced her again. "Excuse me?"

"You keep your feelings about what you do locked inside. You don't share. You don't get over it. You push it down and pretend the bad stuff didn't happen." Running from the piles of emotional baggage drove him. It was as if he'd be smothered if he ever stopped long enough to relax.

His expression went blank. "It sounds like you've given this some thought."

Every single day since they'd been apart. "I'm serious, Connor."

"I can see that."

But he didn't. He watched her and shot back strained responses, but he refused to walk through any of it with her. To give her a chance to shoulder some of the burden and ease whatever doubts and pain twisted in his gut.

She leaned back and rested her head against the wall. "Forget it."

"That's unexpected. You, giving up… Let's just say I'm not used to it." He stared at the ceiling and made a face as if he mulling over his words. "Or I wasn't until you walked out."

The verbal shot knocked into her. Sliced her clean through.

She needed air. Standing up, she brushed by him on the way to the cave entrance. "How long have you been waiting to say that?"

"Whoa." He caught her arm and spun her around to face him.

Even though it was childish and stupid, she wanted to look anywhere but at him. Not give him the satisfaction. "Something else you want to add?"

"I shouldn't have said that."

Not that she didn't deserve it. He meant that he should have tamped his anger with her down inside as well. He didn't say it, but she knew that's where his mind wandered.

"I left because I felt suffocated." Because she wanted to get his attention and make him understand.

"You already told me that."

"Forget it. It's fine." With the verbal jabs and the hours of uncertainty on top of months away from each other, they were anything but.

Still, tearing every sentence apart wouldn't get them anywhere. Not now.

"I give you broad outlines about my work but don't unload because I don't want the garbage from all I see and have to do touching you." His hands rubbed up and down her arms. "I've already mixed everything together by having the office in the house and keeping up a steady stream of houseguests when the guys from the team need somewhere to stay."

"Yeah, so?" The full house, the men coming in and out... That part worked for her. Connor and the guys filled in the pieces of family she'd lost. Having them around, whether they were studying and talking or taking time off and joking, was a bonus, not a burden.

His mouth dropped open. "So?"

"I want the team at the house. That was the deal to keep you close to home and I'm fine with it."

"Really?"

"Of course." When he continued to stare at her, she tried again. "They're family. I wouldn't just tolerate people coming in and out. I would tell you if it were a problem. It's not."

"Probably true but you have to admit the way we live isn't normal."

"Do you think anything about our lives is? We met when you rescued me from a kidnapping. We're together now because someone grabbed me and demanded you come for me."

Darkness passed over his expression. "I realize I put you in danger."

She saw the wall of guilt coming at her and couldn't duck in time. The tension wound around her but didn't push out her frustration. "You're not listening to me."

His hold tightened. "I'm standing right here."

"But you're not hearing what I'm saying."

That jaw clenched and his eyes bulged. "Not for a lack of trying."

She broke out of his hold. "You are as difficult now as you were when I left."

"Is that why you took off? My crappy personality?"

Everything circled back to their separation. It was informal and meant to be temporary, but it had stretched into something else. They'd talked through the same issues—her claustrophobia at being watched every minute, his tendency to shut off. Round after round and still they couldn't wipe it all away and start over.

He talked in generalities and shouldered the blame. But underneath she sensed something else. In reality, she'd waited for this moment since she opened her eyes in the shack and saw him crash through the window. She kissed him first. Followed him here, but she knew he'd been storing up his anger and waiting to fire it at her.

Little did he understand, she had a ball of frustration bouncing around her stomach that could rival his. "I left because you wanted to put me in Bubble Wrap."

His head fell forward and confusion showed in every line of his face. "I have no idea what that means."

She sighed because it was either that or scream. "Yes, you do."

"What I know is my feelings for you haven't lessened one bit."

Between the vibration in his voice and the focused stare, her heart galloped. The longing and need rushed over her but she beat it back. This was too important to just drop and move on.

They'd tried an entire marriage of that and she needed something more. "You're changing the subject."

"I'm taking advantage of ten minutes of quiet before the sun rises and we have to face whatever is stalking us out there to let you know that you've always been the one."

With that, her control shattered. "How could I say no to that kind of sweet talk?"

"You like that, do you?" His hand trailed up until it landed behind her neck. His fingers massaged the tight knot there. "Then you might really enjoy this."

He leaned in and she didn't fight it. Through the bubbling emotions and all the energy swirling around them, this was right.

His mouth brushed over hers, lightly at first. Teasing and coaxing. His tongue ran along her bottom lip then slipped inside. This close, the kiss turned deep and hard, hot and demanding. His lips crossed over hers as his hands roamed all over her head and shoulders.

Heat flashed around her and her knees buckled. One more pass of his mouth and her stomach tumbled. She lost control right along with her inhibitions. Fingers slid into his soft hair and she clenched him tighter against her. Everywhere their bodies touched his skin singed hers.

The kiss turned from gentle to consuming before one thought could pass to another. The timing was wrong but his body and mouth felt so right. It took another few seconds for her to step back. She got as far as lifting her head and resting her cheek against his.

"Well, that was pretty great." His voice came out as a rasp.

She rubbed her face against his. "Always."

"Any chance you want to do it again? Maybe try it without clothes this time?"

Just about every minute of every day. But the team was out there somewhere, along with trained killers and the answers to what had their lives turned upside down. They needed to handle all of that before they could tackle their marriage and all the fun parts that went along with it.

Finding a last pool of inner strength, she broke contact and actually stepped away from him. "Yes, but we need to get back to find satellite access and make sure the rest of the guys are okay."

"I hate when you're reasonable." He exhaled. "But agreed."

His hands kept sliding over her back and igniting a fire in her nerves. She cuddled in closer, enjoying that last second before the intimacy stopped and all their problems came flooding back.

"And I need a gun." She almost laughed when his hands stilled against her. "What? You're the one who insisted I have all that weapons and safety training."

"Practice only."

She lifted her head and stared up at him. "What exactly was I practicing for?"

"I hate that you need to use those skills."

"Then you married the wrong woman, because I am not about to sit back and let the people I love walk into danger without me. That includes you and the team."

He wasn't the only one in this marriage willing to put a body in front of the person he loved. Maybe some of his rescuing vibes got to her, but whatever the reason she had no intention of letting him get hurt. Being shot was more than enough.

"Love."

Jana rolled her eyes to let him know her patience was wearing thin. "Don't act like you don't know I love you."

He shrugged. "It's nice to hear it."

They said it every time they talked on the phone, but she could see the relief cross his face now. For a second the lines around his eyes and mouth eased.

That's why she felt bad about what she was about to say. "Just so you know, if you pull the hero crap and try to take another bullet for me, I'm going to hit you."

He made a face. "Right."

"I'm not kidding."

"Okay, now I've stopped being calm."

For some reason that actually soothed the jumpiness inside her. "It's about time."

Chapter Six

It was times like these that Holt wished he carried a badge. You knocked on the door at six in the morning and flashed official ID and people opened up. You stood there dressed in black with a gun strapped to your side while insisting there was a problem and people got agitated.

This Marcel guy fell into the latter category. Jerky movements, darting glances and all. He stood on the other side of the closed screen door to his one-story house and kept a hand clenched around his cell phone. Holt guessed the man had already typed in 9-1-1.

Marcel frowned. "What are you talking about?"

Holt refused to run through the story one more time, so he cut to the highlights. "Someone broke into the charity office and took Jana last night."

The frown deepened. "Why?"

Shane grunted. "Good question."

"That's what we're trying to figure out." And they'd get to it faster if they weren't on an open front porch, like a target for any shooter lingering around out there.

Marcel lived near the charity in a brown stucco house that blended in with its surroundings. Only the small rock garden out front and the mailbox tipped a person off from a distance that someone might live there.

The house sat in an area lined with a few other buildings. Holt knew from the aerial photos and schematics Davis sent a few minutes ago when the communication lines reopened that the property consisted of a main house, an old barn that now substituted as a bunkhouse for charity workers, and a greenhouse turned storage shed. The neighbor's property stood more than six miles away.

"May we come in now?" Shane reached for the door handle as he asked the question.

The lock clicked. "Are you FBI?"

Holt was two seconds away from letting Shane rip the door off its hinges. This Marcel guy managed to be fully dressed at an hour when most people slept. Dark slim pants and a long-sleeve shirt. Give him a tie and he could step into any office building for a meeting.

Tall and fit with a polished look, Marcel spoke with a slight accent and refused to yield any ground. Holt hated the guy on sight.

He went with the one thing that should shut Marcel's wariness down. "We work with Connor."

Marcel didn't frown so much as grimace, as if he'd tasted something sour. "Jana's husband? I thought they broke up."

"No," Shane shot back with the answer.

Holt didn't blame his friend for the reaction. Something about Marcel's words grated. "They are very much married."

Shane kept glaring. "You might want to keep that in mind."

That had Marcel sputtering. "Meaning?"

Now was not the time for threats. Holt figured they could get to that later. Right now they needed some intel and this guy's shifting and avoidance of questions said a lot. "Jana and Connor are together. End of story."

Some of the color leeched out of Marcel's face. "But she's been here. With me..."

The expression, the comments—it all struck Holt as wrong. "Oh, really?"

"I didn't mean—"

Shane took a step closer to the door. "Anything else you want to say about their marriage and your thoughts on it?"

Marcel cleared his throat. "Where is she now?"

This time Shane rolled his eyes. He looked two seconds away from reaching through the screen and strangling this guy. "With Connor."

"So, she's safe?"

Holt wasn't about to give away her location or engage in a long conversation with this guy about Connor. Holt had no idea what was happening or what the panicked looks from Marcel meant. None of it mattered. Holt's focus stayed on keeping Jana safe. "Can you think of any reason anyone would want to hurt Jana?"

"Never. That doesn't make any sense."

Shane never stopped scanning the area. "But it happened before."

"What did?"

This wasn't a secret. They all knew how Jana and Connor met. How Connor saw her and left his old life behind.

When Jana talked about those days her eyes got all soft and her voice changed. She clearly viewed it as romantic. Connor was much more practical—he saw her, saved her, fell for her then married her. End of story.

Holt decided to take a quick look down memory lane for Marcel's benefit. "This is the second time someone tried to take Jana. The second time Connor stepped in and rescued her."

Marcel's jaw tightened to the point of snapping. "An

entire team saved her the first time. He just happened to be in the lead."

Now that was interesting. Mostly in a this-guy-needed-a-hard-punch way, but seeing anger creep across his face said something. Holt didn't like that. "I sense you're not a fan of Connor."

"I didn't say that."

"Didn't have to," Shane mumbled.

"She's been here doing some outreach and checking invoices. Getting us up to date." When neither Shane nor Holt talked, Marcel stammered and sputtered until he choked out more information. "You know, looking at the paperwork and making sure everything matches."

That time it was what he didn't say that caught Holt's attention. "Does it?"

Marcel shrugged. "There are the usual mathematical errors."

Shane stopped scanning the area and his head snapped back to face Marcel. "Someone can't count boxes?"

"The shipments are larger than that." Marcel stared at his phone then back to the men on the porch again. "Can I see her?"

"No." Shane said it before Holt could even open his mouth.

"Why not?"

Seemed obvious to Holt. "She's with her husband."

"What you can do is let us search the charity office," Shane said.

"For what?"

"Evidence." Holt thought that should end the conversation.

Not a single car had passed by as they stood there. The road appeared abandoned as the only signs of life in the area remained there in the quiet morning arguing about nothing.

Holt liked privacy and quiet but this was creepy. He could see why Connor hated Jana being here. The isolation, Marcel… There was nothing good happening here.

Marcel muttered something then started talking. "I don't think—"

"Enough." Holt barked out the word then forced his seething to calm. "You want to know who tried to hurt her and why, right?"

"Of course."

Shane nodded in the direction of the family room behind Marcel. "Then go get whatever you need to leave."

The man nodded, then slammed the door, trapping them outside. Holt waited until he heard footsteps going away from the door to ask the question burning through him. "Thoughts on this guy?"

Shane dropped back to lean against the wall and face the empty street. "There is no way Jana left Connor for him."

Without picking the subject, Shane had known exactly where Holt was going with the simple question. Connor never talked about Marcel or worries of infidelity but the way he'd reacted to Marcel's name when Jana said it during her rescue spoke loud and clear.

This Marcel guy had somehow wormed his way into the middle of Connor's marriage. Holt wasn't sure how, but an affair struck him as wrong. "I don't think so, either."

"But I get why Connor has a problem with this guy being near his wife."

"Does he look as lovesick as he sounds?" Davis's voice broke in over the comm.

"That and evasive." Holt had forgotten Davis was there, listening in.

With communication restored, Davis refused to be cut

out now. He'd told them Joel worked all night to get them back online. For now, it worked.

Davis snorted. "The math thing?"

"What was that about?" Shane asked.

There were a lot of possibilities, none of them good in Holt's view. "We'll find out soon enough." In the meantime they had a bigger problem, like a missing boss. "You figure out a way to reestablish contact with Connor?"

"Joel is working on it." There was a jumble of male voices over the line. Davis talked louder and rose above the din. "Something about reprogramming the watches."

Shane pretended to cough. "Geek."

Davis laughed. "I'll let him know you think so."

"While you're at it, open a file on this Marcel guy." There was something there. Something big. Holt would bet his life on it.

Papers shuffled on the line before Davis came back on. "Looks like Connor already has one."

Of course he did. Connor prepared for every contingency and didn't leave anything to chance. It was one of the reasons Holt liked his boss and this team so much. "Then let's start digging."

Chapter Seven

Connor tried to block out the kiss. Tried and failed. When everything else went wrong in their marriage, that part burned as bright as ever.

He loved to touch her, kiss her, take her to bed. Over the past year their frustration boiled over and they argued about things that didn't make sense to him, but the sex still worked. Kissing her still made the anger seep away and his gut clench in anticipation.

She accused him of being too guarded, but with her he laid it all on the line. She got to him like nothing and no one before and that hadn't changed.

She brushed her hands against her pants and joined him at the opening to their hideout. "What's the plan?"

He wanted to store her away somewhere safe. That instinct never went away. Problem was, he didn't have a good solution to their situation now. He didn't know how many attackers they faced or what they wanted.

There were too many variables and no place for her to wait while he figured it all out. At least not here. "My idea is simple. Get to a place with phones and don't get shot."

She nodded as she stared at a fixed place in the distance. "I like it. Sounds smart."

"That's why I'm in charge."

She smiled. "I guess so."

The tentative peace tempted him. He could stay quiet and let the question wriggling its way into his brain drop. Maybe wait until they found a hotel and the attackers were caught.... But he couldn't. "So, about Marcel."

Her mouth flatlined and her head fell back on a groan. "Really? Now?"

This time Connor ignored the jealousy eating at him. Forget Marcel's crush, which made Connor want to kick the guy right back to Belgium or wherever he lived before moving to the United States. His question centered on a much more basic issue.

"Why wasn't he at work when the attackers came?" It ticked Connor off that she was there without a bodyguard or an alarm. All the weapons training in the world didn't mean a thing if a gang of thugs grabbed her before she could reach for a weapon, which is exactly what happened.

And he wasn't there to stop it. No matter how their marriage played out, that would eat at him forever.

"Marcel went home and I stayed back to do some work." She crossed her arms in front of her as her voice grew more clipped.

Confirmation. "In other words, he left you alone."

"Marcel is not my babysitter."

Good thing, since he sucked at it. "And not having one turned out great for you this time around, didn't it? That's my point. It's always been my point."

"He's not a trained assassin. He's not my boyfriend or lover or whatever else you're worried about, either." She turned on Connor, facing him down and never breaking eye contact. "I know you don't trust me—"

"I do." She wasn't the problem. He trusted her not to cheat while they were married but he wasn't clear on whether she still wanted to be.

"We've worked together, just work, and Marcel hasn't even looked at me with an ounce of interest."

"You wouldn't notice if he did."

"Uh, what?"

"Men look at you. They show interest. You're beautiful but you never pick up on the reactions to you." Connor did. All the time. And thought he exercised great restraint in not taking anyone out over it.

The pinched look left her face and the start of a smile played on her lips. "That's kind of sweet."

He guessed it was good one of them thought so. "That men look at you?"

"No." She pushed against his shoulder. "That you still think I'm beautiful."

The world tilted on him. It was as if everything he knew to be true went flying and crashed at his feet. "Wow, I must suck at being a husband."

"How did you get to that conclusion?" Her hand rested against his chest, right over his heart.

"You're stunning. Like, steal-my-breath pretty. I see you and everything else washes away." He lifted her hand and kissed her palm. "The idea you don't know that or how much you mean to me tells me I'm as bad at communicating as you say."

"Connor."

Before she could respond or he could ruin the moment by saying the wrong thing, he leaned in. This kiss wasn't hot or deep. Just a soft brush of his mouth over hers. A promise of more to come. A light touch to let her know he wouldn't push. That he would wait.

He lifted his head and stared down into those big eyes. "There."

Her fingertips skimmed over his chin and the stubble growing there. "What was that for?"

"Just because." Not touching her killed him. The endless fighting exhausted him. "But I'm not getting sidetracked."

He loved when she pushed him and insisted on equal ground in their marriage but when it came to her safety he had to be in charge. And getting her to understand that took its toll on both of them.

One of her eyebrows lifted. "From?"

As if she didn't know. "You shouldn't be working in a building, all alone, in the middle of nowhere."

Her head tilted to the side and her hair fell over her shoulder. "I agree."

No way should he have won that fast. "Okay, I give up. That was too easy and could only mean one thing. I'm being set up for something."

She tapped her fingers against his chest. "Paranoid."

"But not wrong."

"I can admit when you're right."

Anything he said would only mess up the moment so he went for noncommittal. "Uh-huh."

"Now you sound skeptical."

Apparently not as noncommittal as he thought. "Cautious."

She balanced her back against the lip of the stone. The position had her facing him but she kept sneaking glances out over the barren landscape. The dry brush and scattering of trees. A formation of boulders, rocks larger than garages, piled as if someone had dumped them there.

The dirt scraped and crunched as she rolled a stone under her shoe. "I stayed back last night to reconcile vaccine shipments. When I couldn't, I got lost in the work and—"

"Wait." An alarm sounded in his head. "Go back. The vaccine shipments are off?"

"A set amount every so many distributions." She eyed him then. "Yeah, I know what you're thinking."

The problem sounded so familiar it had a nerve twitching in the back of his neck. The charity got the all clear from the international community after some trouble years ago. Marcel commanded respect and donors lined up to help him keep kids healthy and safe.

But this wasn't the first time Connor had heard about an irregularity there. Only Marcel's reputation and positive reports from people on the ground receiving the drugs kept the doors open.

"You mean how the last time that happened someone was syphoning off vaccines and selling them on the black market? Yeah, I'm thinking it." Connor took down the group heading up the scam. One sat in jail and two others had died in a shootout.

That time almost got Jana killed. He'd been there on a job and found her. Rescued her then stayed with her while she got checked out in medical.

She winced. "I figured."

From the start, her intelligence and dedication floored him. Add in the face and spectacular smile, along with a body that had him thinking very unheroic thoughts, and his priorities had shifted almost on the spot.

She'd spent her early life on the road, at her father's side while he helped people. She understood danger and didn't flinch at the black ops work. She'd been the perfect woman in Connor's eyes. Still was.

"The paperwork is off by a fairly inconsequential amount compared to the overall shipments. What we send on one end isn't matching up with what arrives on the other, and..." She'd been talking with her hands but they dropped to her sides now. "Well, I admit it's not random. It's happening at regular intervals."

He wondered if she realized how lame her justifications and explanations sounded and how she circled back to the bottom line fast—there was a problem at the charity.

The same information that would have put him on a plane earlier if he'd known. "I see."

"What do you see?"

Trouble. "What did Marcel say?"

"I just found the problem. He thinks it's a math error." She bit her bottom lip as she looked everywhere but at Connor. "We were going to look over it all today."

"But you were kidnapped first." Connor decided not to harp on the part where she left out this pretty important piece of information before.

Their past tied them together and to the charity. Could be whatever popped up now to cause trouble snaked back to that.

"Are you jumping to a conclusion?" she asked.

One that centered on Marcel and how he was the black hole of disaster, yes. "No."

"Sounds like it."

This is what happened when you loved a smart woman. She didn't fumble around and you couldn't gloss over things. She picked up on every nuance and made every connection. It was hot but in this instance it was also a problem. He'd rather figure out the puzzle and gather the evidence. Because if he implicated Marcel and was wrong, Connor feared he'd lose her forever.

But he did have more information than she did. "I'm guessing something is happening on this end since I know the distribution train isn't being raided."

"How?" When he stayed silent, she poked him in the chest. "Connor Bowen, answer me."

"It's nothing."

"It is almost always something when you say that."

She had a good point there. "I need you to stay calm and listen to me."

"Talk." She ground the word out between clenched teeth.

With one last look at the horizon, he closed down the sensation that something wasn't right out there and focused on her. This whole conversation could go sideways on him and…well, he didn't want to think where that could lead.

"A guy I used to work with, someone who was in on the original raid and rescue with me, is watching over Boundless's operations overseas." Connor said just enough but not so much that she'd go off. Or he hoped that was true but when she didn't blink he grew concerned. "You're staring."

"I'm trying to figure out why you would do that and how furious I should be about it."

"This was a precaution only. You kept contact with the charity and did work for them even back in Maryland. And, for the record, there's no reason to be furious. I was doing what any husband would do."

"You think most husbands would use their overseas contacts for oversight on an international charity?" She shot him a "be serious" look. "Really?"

"This is not—" The black dot he'd been watching moved.

Connor squinted against the sun's rays and concentrated all of his attention on the mark. Yeah, no question about it. The space between the tree and that dot increased. Then the dot shifted again.

Her gaze followed his. "What is it?"

"How did they find us?" He didn't realize he'd said the words out loud until he saw her shoulders tense.

He'd walked for a few hundred feet in the opposite direction, laying an alternative trail then covered all of their tracks. He didn't have wireless or satellite or anything that could connect them to a system of locate them. Yet in the thousands of miles of open land, they'd been followed here.

He didn't get it. "Seems pretty random."

The dots—three of them—moved in a synchronized march. And they were more than dots now. At this distance it was hard to make them out, but the figures looked like men in battle gear. They walked at a good clip and closed the distance fast.

"They are headed straight for us." She patted her hip then looked around.

He assumed she was searching for the extra gun he'd handed her when she asked for protection. She turned and he looked at her butt and her shoes and the answer to how they'd been found clicked in his head. "Come here."

Fast and rougher than he intended, he ran his hands over the outside pockets of her pants and across the collar of her shirt. He felt for any bump or anything out of the ordinary.

She tried to pull away from him. "What are you doing?"

"Looking for a tracker."

She grabbed his hand. "You mean…"

"Yes."

He heard a rip and the protective vest fell to the ground. The shirt came next, leaving her wearing only a thin camisole. She slid her fingers around the waistband of her pants and kicked off her shoes. When her body tipped and she lost balance, he grabbed on, keeping one eye on her and one on the men coming over the ridge and right for them.

His pulse pounded and blood thundered in his ears. He didn't panic. The energy soaring through him fueled him. He'd need the adrenaline rush in order to wipe out the wall of attackers heading toward them.

He also needed her out of the small cave. Trapped in there she didn't stand a chance.

"Move." Grabbing the extra gun off the ledge and

the vest and shoes off the ground, he pulled her out of the space and led her down the long tunnel of rocks that opened to the wide expanse of brush at the far side.

She turned and held out her hand. "Shoes."

Lights bounced around them and he could see an escape ahead where she could crawl out. He put the extra gun in her hand as she stumbled around putting the shoes back on. "Take this and use it if you need to. Do not hesitate."

If she stayed low and ran, she could find another place to hide. Everything depended on the timing. If there were other men around the side, she could get caught. If he couldn't hold them off or shoot them down, she might not get away. But first they had to find that tracker.

She'd scooped up her shirt as they went. Her hand clamped up and down the material as she searched. When her gaze lifted and traveled over his shoulder, she moved even faster. "They're coming."

"I'll handle them." He pulled out his gun and gave her one last look. "Find it."

She tucked the weapon in the waistband at the back of her pants. "What will you be doing?"

"Shooting." He turned away from her then. Seeing the worry in her eyes would slow him down. And he needed her on the move.

Less than a minute later, the first bullet pinged by his head. The next lodged in the rock by his shoulder. He flipped back, hiding behind the edge of the cave opening. With a quick glance, he looked down the tunnel and didn't see her. In his mind he had to believe she got away. Now it was his turn.

Shadows moved and footsteps shuffled around him. The gravel made it tough for them to move in quietly, and that was his advantage. Gunfire rang out around him, chipping stones and kicking up a combination of dust and dirt. He ignored it all, biding his time.

When the first man tried to slip around the corner and angle in, Connor nailed him in the head with a bullet. The guy went down in a whoosh. His gun fired and the bang echoed around Connor, but he stayed focused.

One down. Two to go.

He'd just had the thought when a second man popped up in front of him. Connor fired without thinking. The bullet hit the attacker's shoulder and spun him around. The second one went through his neck. The man let out a yell as his hand went to the wound.

As the man fell to the ground, Connor heard a scrape behind him. He turned out to be a beat too late. Before he could shift, shoulders nailed him in the back and knocked the air out of him. He grabbed for the side of the rock in order to stay on his feet but something whacked into his shoulder blades and had him doubling over.

Connor heard the cock of the gun. He stayed down, waiting for the right moment.

"You're lucky the boss wants you alive." The guy leaned in. "Your woman won't be so lucky."

Connor lifted his elbow and slammed it into the guy's jaw. He heard a crack and a roar of anger. Before the man could fight back, Connor went in low, pounded into the guy's stomach and pushed him back into the rock wall.

Punches flew as both men kicked and clawed. Fingernails dug into Connor's flesh through his pants then a hand jerked him behind the knee and off his feet. He felt the warm air rush around him as he went down.

He shifted, trying to spare his back, and his butt and palm took the brunt of the freefall. He hit the hard surface and his gun went flying. It skidded right out of his hand. Lunging for it, he reached out but the attacker beat him to it.

They fought for the weapon, rolling in the dirt, but neither got a good grip. Missing it, Connor settled for pushing it farther away from the other man's grasp.

An elbow rammed into Connor's stomach as he tried to catch the other man's head and pound it into the ground. They flipped and the man's weight crushed him.

Hands, legs—he used it all to gain leverage. The air filled with grunts and moans. The shuffling of their clothes and bodies against the pebbles drowned out every other sound.

In desperation, Connor reached for his knife. The move left him vulnerable for a second and the guy moved in. He punched once, twice into Connor's stomach, causing him to bend over double.

In the battle, the attacker ended up on top, pinning Connor to the dirt as the guy reached over and grabbed his gun. Connor hadn't even realized there were two free for the taking until one filled the attacker's hand.

"I'm going to enjoy your wife before I kill her. Just wanted you to know that." The guy's smile was feral. Sick.

Rage swept through Connor. The thought of Jana being at this guy's mercy gave Connor the push he needed. He gathered all of his energy for one last push. The simple plan lacked finesse—nail the guy between the legs, turn him over and shoot him in the head.

"No, you're not."

Jana's voice had them both turning. The attacker stilled and Connor reached for the gun. Jana beat him to the shot. She fired once and the attacker dropped.

Dead weight fell against Connor. He shoved and pushed until he rolled the guy off.

After a quick check for a pulse, Connor looked up at his

wife. She had her feet planted and her arms up, still aiming as the smell of hot metal surrounded her.

Scrambling to his feet with the aches and soreness fading into the background, he stood beside her and lowered her arms. He had the gun out of her fingers but couldn't get the stiffness out of her hands. "You okay?"

Her body shook with the force of the aftermath. "Not really."

"You saved me." The fact stunned him, leaving him humble and grateful and more in love with her than he'd ever been. And that was saying something.

She finally blinked. "All your training paid off."

As gently as possible, he put a hand on her chin and turned her to face him. "Thank you."

Those beautiful eyes cleared. "I couldn't let him hurt you."

He kissed her forehead because it was killing him not to. "You didn't."

"Okay," She leaned into him as she nodded her head. Every few seconds a tremor ran through her.

He held her through it all. Reality would smack into her later. Taking a life would imprint on her. She did it for the right reasons and didn't have a choice, but she'd need to work through it.

He just wanted her to hold it together now. "You're okay now."

"I found this." She pulled a small black square out of her front pants pocket.

"Nicely done." He dropped it to the floor and ground it under his heel. "And now it's gone."

"I don't recognize any of them." Her fingers tightened in his shirt. "Get us out of here."

Chapter Eight

Luc lowered the long-range binoculars as his first man went down in the distance. The shuffling moved out of position but it didn't start out well. He stood with Bruce, Rich and Reno more than five hundred feet away and out of sight. Keeping Reno from rushing in fell to Bruce. He whipped out a knife to make his position clear.

As they listened in on the radio and minutes passed, Luc heard grunts and shots. Gunfire echoed through the canyons. The men they sent in were too busy fighting to give a status report. They didn't call out directions or ask for reinforcements. They clearly thought they had the situation under control and for a few seconds, Luc believed them.

Then silence. Whispered voices and nothing more. Absolutely nothing that sounded like an all-clear signal.

Reno shoved Bruce's hand away. "What the hell was that?"

"Failure." Bruce's comment said it all.

Luc had been in the business a long time. He worked for the boss off the books. He carried out plans and made sure the shipments moved smoothly. Someone else handled the stupid paperwork. They were supposed to, anyway. But a mess up there trickled down to Luc and now he had a disaster on his hands. A woman who wouldn't stop digging and never seemed to be where he needed her to be.

The boss was going to be ticked off. He didn't like incompetence and he hated Connor Bowen. Losing to Connor and his team would set the boss off. Have him looking for someone to blame. Luc vowed to put Bruce in the firing line. He was the boss's muscle and he couldn't get trained men to do a simple job.

It all came down to Jana. Something about her inspired loyalty in the Corcoran Team. Her husband put his body in front of hers once. He'd do it again. For Luc, that meant killing her was his first priority.

They just had to follow Connor and Jana and figure out the perfect time to swoop in. "Where are we?"

Rich stared at the black box in his hands. It was larger than a cell phone. The green light tracked Jana's movements. That one of the men managed to sneak it on her was a triumph in an otherwise flawed operation.

But then Rich's arms dropped and he started swearing. "Unbelievable."

Luc braced his body for more bad news. "What is it?"

"The tracker's dead."

"How is that possible?" Reno asked, the shock evident in his voice. The big man's face had turned bright red and his cheeks puffed in and out.

Bruce exhaled as he put his knife back in its sheath. "Connor Bowen."

No, it wasn't just him. It was all of them. Luc recognized the extensive prep work and admired it. Every last one of them had resources that put his own men to shame. "His wife is turning out to be pretty resourceful, as well."

Rich threw the box against the ground. The plastic shattered and pieces flew. "Damn it."

Reno got right up in Luc's face. "I told you we all needed to go in."

Holding on to his temper and not letting the bigger man

see any panic, Luc tugged his shirt out of Reno's fists and stepped back. "And risk having Connor and his team take everyone out?"

"He's not some freak of nature," Reno said. "He can't protect his wife and shoot us all."

Rich stopped pacing long enough to wipe his mouth. Whatever was going on in his head had his shoulders tightening. "Who says he's alone? Maybe he met up with his team again."

That was the only piece Luc knew he had covered. "Not possible. We have eyes on them. They aren't out here running around and shooting."

No, that was Connor and his wife. A two-person killing machine. More information that would have been helpful to know a week ago when this operation moved from the planning stages to implementation.

"Are we ready to stop underestimating Connor Bowen?" Bruce's firm voice cut through the anxiety building around them.

Luc would not make that mistake twice. "I want his wife out of this right now."

Bruce's mouth twisted and he looked like he was considering the options. "That probably means killing her."

Fine. The boss might want live bodies but experience said that couldn't happen. Connor would fight to the end. Neutralizing him, ripping out his emotional center, depended on Jana. Kill her, destroy him.

New orders ran through Luc's head and he ticked them off. "Hunt them down. Shoot Connor if you have to, but leave him alive long enough for the boss to talk to him. You can do whatever you want with her."

Rich raised his head and pinned Luc with a glare. "About that—I think we need to meet this boss of yours."

"Do your job." Bruce delivered the comment then started a weapons check. Knives, a gun. He touched everything.

The display clearly didn't impress Rich. He stepped right up to Luc. Barely any space separated them now. "I don't think so."

"You think you'll get more money out of him if you meet him?" If so, Rich didn't understand how the boss operated. He would not be threatened or bribed. He killed people who stepped in his path. Luc could already see a target on Rich's chest.

"I want to know what we're all out here dying for." Rich pointed back and forth between him and Reno. "We're the ones taking all the risk and some guy is sitting in air conditioning somewhere, keeping his hands clean."

There was sharp whack as Bruce thumped his foot against the ground and let his pants leg fall back over the gun strapped to his ankle. "All you need to know is what he wants done."

Reno shook his head. "We're working under new rules now."

"Exactly." Rich stood next to his friend. Together they formed a wall of raging fury. "I agree with Reno. The rules have changed."

Bruce shifted his weight from foot to foot. "No, they haven't."

Time blurred in front of Luc. Before he could blink, Bruce drew his weapon and fired. A red dot formed on Reno's forehead. His mouth stayed open as his body dropped in a heap to the ground. Down on the rock and right over the edge, rolling through the brush until he came to a stop in an unmoving sprawl.

Rich's hands went into the air and his wide-eyed stare followed his friend's descent. Then he turned and went right for Bruce.

"Try me." Bruce's gun didn't waver and the man didn't show a bit of remorse.

"Why?"

Bruce ignored Rich's question. "Go grab your friend's weapons and anything that can tie him to this operation. We leave in five minutes to find Jana Bowen."

Rich's knees gave out and he bent over with his hands on his thighs. "You killed him."

"Consider it a warning."

A tense silence followed Bruce's comment. The men faced each other, neither moving. It was a standoff between two lethal and very stubborn men. Both held weapons but only Bruce looked ready to pull the trigger and walk away. Rich's gaze kept sweeping down the small hill to where his friend's body lay.

A bloodbath came next and Luc didn't want or need that. "Do it now, Rich."

The hesitation stretched until Rich looked away. He jogged over the rise and slid down through the dry shrubs and wall of small rocks.

"That was a mistake." Luc kept his voice low as he stood next to Bruce.

"Let me worry about that."

The man didn't get it. Someone like Rich sought out revenge. Maybe not today, but it would happen. "You'll have a target on your back now."

Bruce finally broke eye contact with Rich's back and stared at Luc. "Then you better makes sure no one hits it."

JANA WATCHED CONNOR pat down the three bodies. She couldn't go a step closer. In fact, she backed up, taking tiny steps and moving deeper into the overhang of rocks. If she could have wedged her body into the seam and disappeared, she might have.

The stench of death refused to leave her. A slight tremor ran through her hands and her insides seemed to shake and squish. She kept from throwing up, but only barely. Even now the bile threatened to rush up her throat and choke her.

On his knees, Connor held up something in each hand and stared at her. “Satellite phone and radio.”

“Good.” She forced the word out. Balling her hands into fists at her sides kept her from rubbing them over her face in shame.

His gaze traveled over her and his eyes narrowed. “You okay?”

She was the exact opposite. At least her wavy vision had cleared a bit.

His concern registered and she rushed to lessen it. “I will be if one of the items you found works and we can leave this place.”

He jumped to his feet and walked toward her. For some reason she stepped back again. Not out of fear because Connor never scared her, but being wired and jumpy any movement only added to her skittishness. She felt as if she could jump right out of her skin.

“I am so sorry you had to do that. For all you’ve seen and been through.” He didn’t reach for her. Just stood there, watching her with dark eyes filled with worry.

Guilt. He had an awesome case of it and her reaction only heightened the issue. She wanted to reassure him but the words wouldn’t come.

Battling through the pain circling around her, she stood straight when she wanted to curl in a ball. After dedicating her world to preserving health and life, she had taken one.

In her head, she couldn’t make sense of the violence. Looking down, she half expected to see blood staining her hands.

He tucked the phone in his pocket and put the radio under one arm. "He would have killed you."

A shiver ran through her. "I know."

"Listen, you did the right thing. It makes me sick you had to…" His strained voice trailed off. With his hands over hers, he leaned in closer, as if willing her to believe. "I wish I could make this better for you."

Being there, holding her, not pushing or insisting she shouldn't wallow all helped. "I know that, too."

"You'll work through this. Promise."

She thought about the weight he carried and the horrors he didn't share. He always said it was to spare her from hearing and him from having to relive them. For the first time she got it.

"I love you." The words slipped out. Not that they were a secret or something he had to earn. She loved him every minute of every day and being on the edge of death she needed him to know that.

His palm cupped her cheek. "And I love you."

He stood close enough for the radio in his pocket to knock against her hip. "Then work your magic and call for help. My only request is we go somewhere without gunfire or dead bodies."

"Aren't you demanding."

"Hurry up before I add something else to the must-have list."

"Yes, ma'am."

The wink caught her by surprise. A shock of lightness spun through her. She kept her eyes focused on his face and her hand braced against his arm. Glancing just a few feet past his shoulder to the puddle of blood seeping into the dirt would send her flying back to that horrible place in her head. She feared closing her eyes and being overcome by the vivid mental images.

Connor skipped the radio and went for the satphone. He fiddled and pressed buttons. When it beeped several times and then the line clicked, she assumed that was some sort of ring. Hearing Holt's voice had her slumping into Connor's side in relief.

"Holt?" Connor being Connor, he made the connection and started talking. No greetings or small talk. "No time to explain. We had more men on our trail but took care of them."

"How many?"

"Three." Connor didn't mention her shot.

She didn't fill in the blank or take credit. Instead, she focused on the steady rhythm of their deep voices. The sound lulled her into a sense of security.

"They have to be running out of men," Holt said.

"You'd think so, but there always seems to be an ample supply of men of this type."

"True. Is Jana okay?" Holt's usual no-nonsense tone came over the speaker.

"I'm fine."

Connor's eyebrow raised but he didn't comment. "Where are you?"

"Lampari's house."

The news had Jana's stomach plummeting to the hard canyon floor. She wanted to ask why and hear what Holt had found out, but she held it all in. Marcel was the one topic sure to make Connor go nuts and she needed him on his game now more than ever.

"Stay there. And get Davis checking on Boundless. We have some shipment irregularities." Connor watched her as he said the words. "A guy I used to work with can help. He's still black ops, but he had connections and intel. His name is Drake Federson. Have Davis use the dark blue cell phone in my top desk drawer. There's one number but tell him to talk fast."

As she listened, Holt delivered the same information Connor gave her but with a little more detail. Through it all one thing was clear—Connor believed that whatever happened in the charity office was tied to the kidnapping.

She didn't see the connection but it was possible this all stretched back to when they'd met. She couldn't ignore the charity incongruities or the fact Marcel had missed them. Again.

The line crackled before Holt started talking. "You staying under?"

"It's too dangerous for us to be moving around out here. The hired guns could be anywhere, including near you. So watch."

"Of course."

"We'll meet up with you when the sun goes down." Connor gave a quick look around. "If the satphone service goes out, meet at Lampari's yard at nineteen hundred."

"Joel is trying to break through whatever blocked our signal earlier and trace it back to the source."

Connor nodded. "He'll figure it out."

There it was. The absolute certainty in his men's skills. Connor acted as if they could wiggle out of any situation and break any code. He made her believe it, too.

"Out."

She could almost see Holt nod as he broke the connection. The ease with which Holt and Connor communicated settled her nasty case of nerves. The two men didn't get wound up and their confidence strengthened hers.

A boot from the downed man caught her attention and she angled her body to block it again. The temptation to plaster on a fake smile came and went. She didn't have to pretend with Connor. She knew that much.

She folded her arms then refolded them. She finally settled for resting a hand on the top of his belt. "What happens until tonight?"

"We put more distance between us and these bodies."

"I'm all for that."

"Davis will advise the proper authorities and get cleanup out here once the danger dies down." Connor glanced behind him. "We need to identify these men and give them proper burials."

Even with death Connor insisted on dignity. Of the many things she loved about him, his refusal to see the bad guys as less than human was one of them. He would kill and protect but he told her there were limits. She suspected that at some point either he or someone he worked with in the past breeched those limits.

"Until then, we wait out the afternoon." He kissed her forehead.

Heat blasted through her from out of nowhere. The shaking inside her took on a very different feel. Call it adrenaline or a will to live, but in that moment she wanted his arms around her and his mouth on hers. "Interesting."

He must have sensed the change in mood because his body tensed and his head lifted again, nice and slow. "Is it?"

"You, me and a cave?" Her fingers slipped over his scruff, loving the rough feel against her skin. "Not this one, but another one."

"It's too dangerous." But his hands tightened on her waist and his body brushed against hers.

"Absolutely." But it had been so long and her need for him pulsed inside her.

"And then there's the part where we're still fighting."

She kissed his chin. "Not about this. We've always communicated just fine on this level."

"Are you trying to seduce me?" The hand skimming down her back and over her backside said that was fine with him.

Her mouth moved to the space just below his ear. "Is it working?"

"I'll let you know when we get to the cave."

Chapter Nine

Holt stood across from where Marcel sat on his couch. After them pounding on the door and throwing Jana's name around a few times, the guy finally let them in. Reluctantly. He didn't exactly offer up drinks and information. He was too busy staring at the back of his hands.

Footsteps signaled Shane's return from his trip to the bathroom down the hall. His fake trip that covered up his recon. No one could assess and categorize a place like Shane. In a few minutes he could survey the place, take it all in then spit out a description of the setting, down to the books in the bookcase, hours later.

Cam called it a photographic memory. Shane called it a gift he'd never asked for. Either way, it served the team well more than once.

Now he lounged in the doorway between the family room and the hall leading to the rest of the house. His eyes were half closed but Holt knew his friend noticed everything.

Shane had learned to sleep in short bursts. No question he was wide awake and ready for battle. The slight shake of his head said they were alone and he didn't find anything out of the ordinary.

That was a shame. Holt hoped for a quick and not-so-dirty end to this. Looked like they had to push through it the hard way. And that meant cracking this guy.

He could dance around it and work on his subtlety but Holt suspected moving in for the kill would shake up this uptight dude. And Holt wanted to shake him hard. Starting now. “Anything you want to tell us about the charity?”

Marcel’s head came up fast. “Excuse me?”

“Some troubles you forgot to mention, maybe?” Shane managed to look bored and sound menacing at the same time.

Holt wished he had that skill. He tended to jump right to scaring the crap out of people who deserved much worse. Probably had something to do with his size. At six-three he often towered over people and his sister insisted he’d never learned to smile. Another effective tool, but he sensed this guy had information he wasn’t sharing. If whatever this Marcel left unsaid put Jana in danger, Connor wouldn’t have to rip the man apart because Holt would do it for him.

The papers at the charity offices might provide a lead. Cam secured most of them before staking the place out and waiting for the attackers to return. Then again, the whole kidnapping thing could be a ruse to destroy the evidence. If so, a lot of dead bodies littered the ground because of some shipping issue.

That was the kind of nonsense problem guaranteed to get Shane riled. And Holt loved watching that.

Marcel’s back stayed stick straight. “Did Connor tell you I did something wrong?”

Holt glanced at Shane before answering. “What’s your problem with my boss?”

“Nothing.” Between the sneer and the wave of his hand, Marcel’s actions telegraphed the exact opposite.

Shane pushed off from the wall and came to a halt beside Holt. The stark expression suggested Shane was right on the edge of doing something Connor would approve of…and Marcel would hate.

"Head's up here, but you're not convincing." Shane widened his stance. "At all."

"Jana deserves…"

"You?" Holt shot back, hoping to throw this reserved guy off his game.

"Of course not."

"You're fine there." When Marcel stood up, Shane slapped a hand on his chest and pushed him back down. "Now try again."

Marcel's Adam's apple bobbed as he swallowed. "This is about my concern for her."

No question Connor needed to do something about this guy. Something that could involve punching and definitely included a few threats about staying away from his woman.

Holt snorted. "Yeah, concern. Got it."

"You can leave now."

Instead of moving away, Shane crowded in closer to the couch. "You want us to leave you alone? I guess that means you don't mind if the kidnappers come here next."

Marcel had to lean back to look up. "I thought this was about Connor."

An interesting bit of conclusion jumping to Holt's mind. "What 'this' are you referring to?"

"Well…whatever reason Jana is in danger."

Funny how the guy who didn't know anything about the break-in or Jana being taken a few hours ago all of a sudden had a theory. One that pointed away from him and put the blame squarely on someone else.

Holt noticed Marcel didn't assume this was a burglary gone wrong or a random act. No, Marcel tied it all back to Connor. As far as red flags went, this was a pretty obvious one.

"Men stormed into your charity office, blew the place apart and took off. Your business, not Connor's." Shane set out the scenario then stood there, staring. He could go without talking for hours. It wore people down fast. This time he stayed quiet just long enough for Marcel to start squirming. Amazing how that trick of Shane's always worked. Holt vowed to work that one into his repertoire.

"Who's over at the office now?" Marcel asked.

"One of my men." Holt stationed Cam there. The guy could hold his position, not move for hours. The skill made Holt wonder just what the guy did before he threw in with Corcoran. Cam liked to joke but there was a vein of steel underneath.

Marcel shifted. "We should—"

Shane held up a hand, clearly ready to shove the guy down again. "Stay there."

"Why?"

"Reinforcements are coming." Holt didn't like new people and certainly didn't trust some random guy to walk in and clear all this up. But Holt trusted Connor and if he said this Drake person from Connor's past could help, Holt would go along. Be wary but not object.

"The police are taking over?" The color left Marcel's cheeks as he said the word.

"Nope." But the comment drew Holt's interest. Shane must have thought so, too, since he snuck a peek at Holt.

"Who then?" Marcel grabbed on to the edge of the sofa cushion.

Tension whipped through the room. If Marcel hadn't been a suspect before then, he sure was now. Getting anxious at the mention of law enforcement was never a good sign.

The more jumpy Marcel got, the calmer Holt felt.

"We're bringing in a guy who is very familiar with your charity. He's been following your work for a while now."

"I don't know what that means."

Shane smiled in a way that promised a certain type of satisfaction. "You will."

CONNOR KEPT THEM in the shade as much as possible. They trekked over flat rocks and through soft red sand. His calves tightened and the sun burned his exposed skin. He made her wear the protective vest and her shirt underneath despite the heat. Taking off his outer shirt, he had her wrap it around her head for some amount of protection.

Sweat beaded on her forehead. Pieces of hair hung down around her face and every so many steps she dragged her feet. Tired and damp and covered in both of their clothing she still was the hottest woman he'd ever seen. When she made her offer back in the cave he almost lost control. He'd been dreaming about her and missing her. He loved the thought of finally making love with her again, but her timing needed work.

Right now he needed them out of the heat of the day and somewhere less exposed. They couldn't run and didn't see anyone else. It was a slog. One during which he spent most of the time scanning the distance and listening for signs of life from the attacker's radio. It never squawked.

Clearly someone on the other side knew not to give anything away. Again suggesting they were dealing with trained professionals. At least Connor's worries about a novice making wild decisions and opening fire without thinking lessened. If these guys knew what they were doing he might be able to track their potential movements and anticipate them.

"Any idea where we're going, or are we walking around

blind?" She tugged at the neckline of her shirt and waved a hand in her face like a makeshift fan.

"Holt passed along a potential hiding spot from Davis." Using the coordinates and tracking on the satphone, Connor could tell they were almost on top of it.

Somehow they'd made the walk without running into animals of the two- or four-legged kind. No gunfire and no racing from attackers. It was a nice change but the respite didn't fool Connor. Whatever was happening wasn't over.

"Does he spend a lot of time in Southern Utah?" She watched each step with care.

"No, but he can read topography reports and maps. Then he probably had Joel hack into military software and—"

She put an arm across Connor's chest. "Sorry I asked."

They crested a small hill and looked out over the wide expanse of orange and red rubble with brush sprinkled throughout. In the distance a rough rock wall towered high enough to block the view to anything beyond. The uneven surface and slabs jutting out probably qualified as a climber's dream. Connor hoped the opposite side had some shade.

She walked faster now. On her third step she jumped out of a deep divot running in a line along the ground and followed a section of rubble toward a pile of rocks about three feet high.

Something moved and he felt that familiar tick at the back of his neck that signaled danger. "Hold up."

The brown lump blended into a patch of sand. The colors matched the landscape and gave the impression of a group of rocks. But he knew exactly what he was looking at and it wasn't a rock or a twig or anything else. It was very much alive.

She spun around as her hand went to the gun strapped to her side. "What now?"

This could go very badly. He had to tell her and fast because if she spied it first—worse, if it moved—the screaming would bring every guy with a gun within a hundred miles running.

Connor held up his hands and concentrated on lowering his voice as he delivered the news. "Do not move or yell."

"Why?"

"You need to stay calm."

"Now you're scaring me."

He nodded to a spot about ten feet in front of her. "There is a…"

She followed his gesture. Sprinting came next. She was at his side, tugging on his arm and all but climbing on top of him before he could say the word. *Snake.*

After all her traveling and the lessons her father passed on, not much scared her. Spiders, fine. Terrible weather, no problem. Scary highways, heights and tight spaces, all good. Snakes… They were a different story. They terrified her.

Her foot inched up the back of his calf as she curled around him. "This is my nightmare."

Her voice shook and she pushed in even tighter. Glanced all around. Even took out her gun.

The closeness worked for him but he hated to see her fear. "I know."

"Where is it exactly?"

He lowered her weapon and slipped it back into the holster. "Under the rock pile."

"There are a hundred of those. I don't see…" She squinted, then her eyes popped open wide. "Oh."

Even though he doubted she could hear him, he tried

to smooth this out. More information usually eased panic but in this case probably not. "It's a nightsnake."

"It's daytime."

"I think it refers to their preference of staying hidden during the day."

"I don't even want to know how you know that."

"I studied them when you came out here." After they got off the phone he'd spend hours paging through information about Utah. There were all sorts of critters out there. Many he doubted she even thought about but kept him up at night with new worries, but snakes were an issue for her so he studied up. "Looked up a bunch of photos."

Her expression morphed to the what-is-wrong-with-you type. "Because?"

"I know you're afraid of snakes and that snakes are in abundance here, so if you got into trouble and called or sent a photo I wanted to be able to tell you what you could do." He thought he heard a little "ahhh" and figured he'd lost her somewhere in the dry explanation. Probably had something to do with the way her body fit against his and how talking and not thinking kept him from stripping the clothes off her. "What?"

"I'd kiss you if I wasn't afraid of dying."

"You won't die," he assured her. "It's only mildly venomous."

"Mildly?"

That's what the book said. This type of snake slept during the day and was fine so long as not provoked and he had no intention of doing that, even if the snake wasn't a worry for humans. "Yes."

"Is that 'mildly' part really a thing?"

He didn't know how to answer that so he spit out another fact. "The snake prefers lizards to people. We're totally safe."

"Is it wrong that I'm hoping it's dead?" She grabbed on to him even tighter. Wound her arm through his and stood on his foot. "Not in a vicious incident or anything. Like, not a snake hunter, if those exist. Something like old age, but I definitely need him or her, whatever it is, not breathing."

The babbling thing made him want to smile but he didn't dare. "You okay?"

"I don't like snakes."

They tended to fail at communication lately but he got this point. "We'll swing wide and leave him alone."

"What if he has friends or this is like an informal snake town or something?"

"Wow." He made a mental note to hire an exterminator to check the Maryland property every few months or so.

Though the thought of Jana jumping into his arms every now and then certainly didn't bother him. The way her teeth chattered now did.

"I hate snakes."

"Again, noted." He put an arm around her. "I can carry you."

Her fighting spirit came sprinting back. It flashed in her eyes and showed in her frown. "I'm not that pathetic."

A few years of marriage had taught him one thing. There was no right answer to that sort of comment. "Okay."

They had to keep moving, so he guided her around the snake's resting place. Took her way over to the side, nowhere near the suspect bush, all while looking around for more snakes. Thinking they'd survived the rock and tree obstacle course, he walked toward their afternoon hideout.

A few feet out, she stopped. "I would have, you know."

He tried to figure out if he'd missed part of the conversation. "What are we talking about?"

"Called you." She slipped her hand into his. "If I got

into trouble, you are the one I'd cling to. Even with the fighting and wanting to shake you—"

"Thanks."

"I knew I could count on you."

He gave her fingers a squeeze. "Always."

"When the kidnapper called you, I knew you'd come running."

"I would never let anyone hurt you." That was the vow he made when he asked her to marry him.

He'd promised she would always come first. That no matter what, he would keep her safe. But somehow, some way, despite all the precautions and planning, his life had put her in very real danger. Only her smarts and some quick thinking by the team got them out of there without being killed.

She nibbled on her lower lip. "You just hold on so tight."

"And when I didn't, someone grabbed you." That's the failure he could not work around or forget. The flight across the country trying to get to her amounted to pure torture. The fact danger still sucked them under kept the hits coming.

"That could have happened anywhere."

But it happened on his watch. He didn't say it, but he felt it to the bone.

He pointed to the rock slabs and the thin opening between them. "Over here."

She turned sideways and slipped inside. He followed, with his chest and back touching the walls. He was just about to call this off and look for another option, one with some breathing room, when he stepped into the open area. Boulders towered above them, each stacked upon the other. The top was open and blue skies flashed above them. At the far end of the long tunnel of rocks was another opening to the rubble beyond.

The formation created an open space about a third the size of a football field. She stepped into the center and spun around. “This isn’t a cave.”

“We can see a wide swath of land and have multiple ways in and out.” Just as Davis promised. Connor decided his second in command needed a raise. They all did.

She stepped to one side and ran her hand over the colors veining the rocks as she lifted his shirt off her head. “Davis thought about all of that?”

“He’s a good man.” The best, because Connor only hired the best.

“They all are.” She spun around and faced Connor again. Her hair swished. The sun had colored her cheeks. “So are you.”

Gone was the fear of snakes and anguish of all the long, hard hours behind them. The stillness, this beautiful woman and the stark landscape behind her… It all combined to send his pulse racing and his common sense on vacation.

The kick of need hit him so hard he almost groaned in reaction. “You said something about a seduction.”

“Soon.”

“Now works for me.”

She screwed up her lips. “It did for me, too…. Then I saw the snake.”

“I could probably make a gross joke here.” If he could put the words together. Right now his brain locked on permanent misfire. All he could do was feel. Thinking abandoned him.

“The idea of getting naked with snakes slithering around…” She gave a dramatic shiver. “It kind of kills the mood. They could be anywhere, just waiting to attack. I plan on watching out for them and I can’t do that if I’m crawling all over you.”

She just had to use that word. Now the visual image that popped into his mind wouldn't leave. But the snake comment pretty much ended any possibility of getting on his back with her on top of him.

It would happen and she was right that it would be soon. Rock, ground, bed, car. He wasn't picky.

He decided to let her know where his mind had wandered. "You know the first bed we find I'll be all over you."

Heat spun around her and her cheeks flushed. "It's been a long time."

The tension zapping between them had nothing to do with fighting. "Too long."

She took the few steps to close the gap between them. When he opened his hand, she put hers in his. "I need you to know I didn't run to Marcel."

Talk about a subject sure to kill off the last of Connor's sexual thoughts. "You kind of did."

"I'm sorry." Her other hand rested on his chest, right up near his throat. A finger swept over his neck.

The touching and closeness made it tough for him to swallow. "For?"

"Doing the one thing guaranteed to hurt you."

He wanted to look away from the sudden starkness in those eyes. This conversation needed a table and boundaries and plenty of rest before it started. Now was not the best time for this conversation. Too much could go haywire. He could say the wrong thing or pick the words sure to send her running again.

Still, he had to know one thing. He'd never viewed her as deliberately hurtful and couldn't figure out what he'd done that would be so wrong as to invite the sort of emotional stabbing she'd delivered. "Was that the plan? To make me think you wanted Marcel instead of me?"

"No, Connor. I swear. Never that." Her hands traveled over his face and shoulders. "I didn't set out to hurt you."

Relief crashed into him. Intentionally causing pain was not her style. It wasn't who she was or how she operated. He'd hoped and justified her actions on that score. Knowing he got that part right meant something. "Good."

"Please believe me when I say I know I made a mistake." Her hands soothed as they went. "I wasn't thinking and miscalculated, and by the time we fought about Marcel on the phone a few weeks ago I didn't have anywhere else to go."

That was the one thing she kept getting wrong. Very wrong. "You could have come home and worked it out with me."

"Would you have listened?" Before he could respond, she exhaled, giving him the full female treatment from head tilt to sad smile. "See, I think you would have told me what I wanted to hear to lure me back, but then life would have settled back into the same pattern."

The assessment struck a bit too deep. Getting her back made him ruthless. He would have tried any tactic. But the idea that he would have relaxed once she was back home was just plain wrong. Having lost her, he'd do anything not to go down that road again.

Now he had to make her understand that. "You don't have much faith in my ability to change."

"It's not just you. It's us." Her hand slipped up to his cheek. "I am as much to blame as you are. We gloss over problems and they fester. You ignore them and I explode. It's a back-and-forth we need to break."

This counted as the first time she talked in terms of *them* messing up instead of just him. He tucked that away to examine later. "So, where does that leave us?"

"I would never cheat, and I think you know that." Her

hands dropped away and the distance between them widened even though she didn't physically move back. "My feelings for Marcel are really platonic. There's no spark and absolutely no interest on my part."

She'd said things like that before but the way she said it now—so dismissive of there ever being anything else—had some of Connor's anxiety washing away. "I think we should tell Marcel that. Just make sure I'm there to hear it."

"There is only one man I love. You drive me nuts but there is just you." She wrapped her arms around his neck and tugged his head down for a kiss.

Not sweet or soft. This was a clothes-stripping, head-spinning kiss. It sucked him under and had him reeling. When she pulled back, he wanted to keep going. He thought about trying to convince her to forget the snakes and the danger and let him touch her.

But he wasn't that guy and she deserved a better reconciliation. "Wait until we get to that bed."

Chapter Ten

Connor's sensual promise still rang in her ears hours later. They'd rested most of the day. Well, she did. He guarded. Paced around and turned at every sound. When she closed her eyes she thought about snakes, so she dozed on and off, jerking awake from time to time, listening for a rattle or whatever the nightsnake did before it attacked.

Now they stood behind trees, hiding as they watched the front of Marcel's house. The sun had started to fade and a single light on the porch highlighted the red door and cast the rest of the place in shadows. They blended into the landscape. She could make out other buildings and see most of the yard thanks to a bright light on the side of the makeshift bunkhouse.

Connor had told her about the sensor lights and how to dodge them. She didn't really get the plan. Up until ten minutes ago she thought she knew it. Meet up with Holt, Shane and Cam, regroup and try to find some answers. All while avoiding guns and explosions.

Still they stood there. Watching.

She glanced over at Connor. Leaning into a trunk, he held his large body still and focused on a spot in the middle of the yard. Whatever he saw had him frowning.

Impatience walloped her. "I give up."

He didn't break his eye contact with the unseen issue only he saw. "What?"

"What are we doing?" She whispered because he did, but she was just about done with ducking and mumbling.

She wanted her life back. All of it. Annapolis, her house, Connor…safety. Problem was she didn't see a clear road that led from where she was now to all she hoped to gain.

"We're waiting," he said.

The man sure did have a grasp of the obvious. "Apparently."

He looked at her then. "I need to know it's safe before I take you up there."

"We heard from Holt a half hour ago and he gave you the all clear." She pressed both hands against the tree and felt the rough edges dig into her palms.

"I know."

"Well, that clears up your plan."

Connor exhaled and looked inches away from a frustrated-male eye roll. "Jana—"

She rushed to shut that down. "Don't even think about it."

He frowned. "What?"

"The lecture or whatever it is you want to say." She held up a palm. "Save it."

"Fine." He took her hand and spun her around. Shifting positions, he now stood behind her. One arm rested on her shoulder. With the other, he pointed. "See the brown tarp about a hundred yards off to the right of the house? It keeps moving. It's very slight, but it shakes."

She squinted, even closed one eye, but she didn't see it. Good thing she trusted him to notice things like that. "Maybe the wind?"

"There isn't any."

She glanced over her shoulder. It was only then she

realized they were on top of each other. His heart thumped against her back and his strong arms wrapped around her.

"What are you thinking?" She knew what she was thinking and it didn't have much to do with a tarp.

"Trap." He pressed a palm against the tree in front of her face. "Normally I'd head over and check it out, but I'm not leaving you alone."

She turned until she faced him, rested in his arms with him all around her. "You just rush in when you think there's a trap?"

"I'm in charge. It's my job."

The response wasn't a surprise. The man she knew wouldn't sacrifice someone else. He wasn't the kind of boss who sat in a room and issued orders from a safe distance. He was a boots-on-the-ground type of guy.

But she needed him alive because the thought of any other option washed the life right out of her. "Add that to the list of things we're talking about when we sit down for our relationship chat."

He frowned. "Danger on the job can't be a surprise."

"It's the way you welcome it that scares me."

"I don't—"

A male chuckle broke Connor's concentration. Davis's voice came through the earpiece a second later. "Wanted to break in and welcome you back to the comm. Also remind you now that we're back up and running we're all listening in, but feel free to be embarrassing."

"Thanks."

Jana shook her head. "Why are you thanking me?"

Connor remembered she couldn't hear the conversation. With his team and their somewhat loose sense of boundaries, that might turn out to be a good thing. "I'm not."

"You just said—"

"It's nothing."

"Okay."

Holt groaned over the line. "Or you could just tell her the truth. That we're right here, except in body."

Despite the rapt audience, Connor wanted to make one thing clear. He spent years working undercover for his country. Back then he followed the rules and didn't question authority. In operation after operation he experienced unrelenting violence. Engaged in it and witnessed it until he thought he'd never get clean.

The case files flipped through his brain. All that paperwork for jobs no one was supposed to know about.

When he was told to ignore atrocities in the name of collecting data and growing intel, he balked. By the tenth time, he grew disillusioned. And years ago when he saw a man put a gun to Jana's head as he made her plead for her life, Connor realized the urge to kill had become ingrained in him.

Back then he hadn't wanted justice for her, he wanted revenge. At that time he only knew her name because the file listed it but the urge to fight for her already slammed into him pretty hard.

Throughout his time with her, first the hours then the weeks and eventually the months, he changed. Watching the way she cared about people and fought to move vaccines to the populations that desperately needed them, reordered his priorities. She could hold a conversation with the person behind her in line at the grocery store. Her life didn't depend on her hiding in the shadows. That freedom intrigued him and he sought it out.

He'd made a conscious decision to get out of the work that stole his humanity and never regretted it. Detaching was not easy. He went through days of training and psychological testing to make sure he wasn't a threat to the agency he'd always served. They'd gone round and round until he promised to provide assistance from his new life in security.

The first few assignments for the new firm revolved around agency cases. It wasn't until his fourth kidnap rescue with Corcoran that his superiors finally and officially let him go.

So, no, he didn't seek out danger. He walked away from a life mired in it. "I don't."

"What?" she asked.

"Like danger."

She actually smiled. "Come on. You thrive on it."

"I do what I do to stop it."

Her face fell. "Do you really believe that?"

He didn't get her reaction but that didn't change his response. "I have to."

"We have company." Holt spoke this time.

Connor knew then Holt had been staking out the yard, watching and assessing. "The tarp."

She poked his chest. "Why do you keep saying random words?"

Connor tapped his ear. "We're back up and ears are everywhere."

"At least for a few minutes." Holt continued the attacker report. "And we have two at the back of the house, coming around the porch."

"So, we have three incoming total?" Connor expected more of an armed presence.

"You really must have ticked off the guy in charge because he sure is determined to get you," Holt said.

"I have that effect on people."

Connor blinked and Jana's face loomed in front of him. "Stop talking to them and talk to me. What are we going to do?"

"Smoke the bad guys out."

But that plan fizzled when Connor saw the men sliding along the side of the house. He whispered the word sure to get everyone inside moving. "Dark."

Shifting her behind him, Connor moved back and farther away from the light. She grabbed fists full of his shirt and he knew she sensed the danger. He didn't have to yell a warning or give directions. She still had her gun but this time he didn't want her to use it.

If there was shooting to do, he'd do it. The stain of every person he'd ever killed stayed with him, but he'd learned to live with it. He didn't want her to carry that burden.

The tarp fluttered and when Connor looked back at the house the two men had made it to the front porch. He wanted to take a photo for Joel and Davis to work from, but there was no way Connor would lower his weapon or be that vulnerable just to get an ID.

One of the guys lined up with the front window. He shifted and peeked inside. Whatever he saw had him scooting back and out of the line of sight from inside. The second one ducked and ran under the window until they took up space on each side of the glass.

Connor called on his training, trying to make out their faces, but they turned away. They stayed focused on the inside of the house. Other than their builds and hair color, he couldn't give much of a description.

"Stay here." He gave the order but didn't move until Jana nodded.

Even then he didn't go far. He switched trees, trying to get a better angle. He flattened his back against the bark and glanced over at her. She had her body pressed up against the tree. Slim and still. No one would notice her unless they already knew she stood there.

If either one of these guys fired inside, any one of his

men could be hit. If the team fired, a stray bullet could hit Jana. Connor couldn't risk that.

Marcel, the team… They all needed to get out without bloodshed. Making that happen was the issue. Being out front made hiding his approach tough. But that's exactly what he had to do.

With one last warning look in Jana's direction, Connor took off. He ignored the swift shake of her head and the fear in those eyes. Holt would have everyone inside away from the windows, but depending on how natural he wanted them to look, people could be in that front room.

Just then Holt's voice whispered over the line in a sound so low Connor almost thought he imagined it. "In three."

"Jana is in the line of fire."

After a brief hesitation Davis came on the line. "No fire."

"Understood." Holt's flat voice didn't question. "Three…"

The countdown filled Connor's head. Looked like they weren't waiting and these intruders didn't plan to move without a fight. Connor was happy to oblige. He dropped low to the ground, trying to figure out if that angle would hide him. Without the rocks and scraping of his shoes, maybe it would work. But he needed leverage and silence.

"Two…" Holt continued the counting. "One…"

Connor sprang up on *go* and his shuffling had the men outside at the front door turning in his direction. For a second, he got a solid look. Tall, deadly and that's all that registered.

The front door slammed open and the shouting started. Footsteps thudded on the wooden porch as the attackers scrambled.

Holt called out directions and someone streaked across the grass. A single gunshot from the lawn started an explosion of firepower. The rat-a-tat-tat filled the air and noises pinged all around him. Glass shattered and rocks kicked up as the team dropped out of sight. The display worked as cover and let the attackers move out as fast as they came in.

All shots came from outside. Holt clearly kept the team from firing near Jana. Connor appreciated the protection but hated not being able to just knock the attackers out.

By the time he hit the side of the porch, Connor saw that the men had disappeared. Literally. With his speed and skills, the attackers still got away, likely believing the offensive strike they launched had worked.

Connor visually searched the area and didn't see any sign of the attackers. Darkness or not, he couldn't spot shadows or movement. It was as if they vanished into nearby stones, which made no sense at all.

He kept one eye on his men and the other on Jana where she'd squatted down and huddled by the tree. If the attackers had known she sat there, she'd likely be gone. He called out to her to come to him. After a second or two of hesitation she jumped up and raced until she landed at his side.

He wrapped an arm around her while he held his gun with the other. "You okay?"

"You should stop asking that until we're safe."

Holt chuckled from his position in the middle of the front doorway. "We all good?"

Jana tugged on Connor's shirt. "You guys didn't shoot."

He didn't want to go into tactics and strategies now. The inability to grab at least one of the attackers had fury burning in his gut. "The area was too uncontrolled."

"You mean you thought I'd get hit in the crossfire."

Holt answered. "Yes, Jana, and we'd play it the same way again."

"And I'm sure we'll have another chance to make an offensive strike." Coming to this house, right to the porch, meant the attackers either believed in their invincibility or were operating in panic mode. Connor didn't like either possibility but at least he knew how to plan for each.

"I don't understand." Marcel appeared over Holt's shoulder. "What was that?"

"Pure defense, which is not our favorite thing so now is not the time to be annoying." Shane dragged the older man outside to the porch.

Holt pulled Marcel the rest of the way outside. "Speaking of which, any reason you put on your shoes and kept staring at the windows during the last hour?"

"What are you talking about?" Marcel broke from both men's holds the minute his gaze locked on Jana. "You're here. I'm so relieved."

Before Connor could stop it or Jana could say hello, Marcel grabbed her in a crushing bear hug. If that went on more than two seconds, Connor would have to put his gun down to keep from using it.

Jana made the decision for him when she broke away. She didn't just step back. Her voice turned chilly and she folded her arms in front of her.

That didn't stop Marcel from putting a hand on each of her shoulders. "You're okay."

"She is for now." *And no thanks to this guy.* As far as Connor was concerned, Marcel opened the door to danger and touching his wife just invited more.

"What is that supposed to mean?" Marcel asked.

The backbone was new. Connor remembered Marcel as being quiet and charming to the point where Connor wanted to pound him. Here he showed more emotion. Maybe he'd finally stopped pretending his feelings for Jana centered only on friendship. If so, his timing was worse than hers.

"You're a little late to step in with the concern, aren't you?" Connor asked.

Jana turned to Connor. She put a hand on his stomach. It was a gentle touch but it carried a loud warning for him to behave. "Now is not the time for this. We've all had a long day."

"Understatement." Shane offered his insight as he stepped to the edge of the porch and looked into the darkening night.

"We need to regroup and talk, and I'm volunteering your kitchen." Holt pointed toward the inside of the house.

The plan made sense to Connor but there was one man missing. "Where's Cam?"

"At the charity offices."

"Keep him there." The guy needed a break but, knowing Cam, he wouldn't agree to one. If Connor assigned Cam somewhere, Cam stayed until the job was done.

And there was no question this case was not over. Men crept around everywhere.

Jana made a face. "Doesn't he need some sleep?"

"No." But Connor liked her show of concern for the men.

She'd always been like that. It matched her caring nature to take in strays from the team. She's find extra pillows and make them comfortable, never knowing almost all of them had served time in the military or black ops and could sleep in a tree, if necessary.

After one last lingering look in Jana's direction, Marcel turned and went inside. Connor found the man totally annoying but didn't say it out loud. From the look of Shane's and Holt's glares into Marcel's back, Connor guessed he wasn't alone.

One by one they walked into the house. Connor hooked an arm around her and guided them to the doorway. He wanted them out of sight as soon as possible even though he sensed the attackers were long gone. They snuck away somehow and he doubted they'd return immediately after their successful escape.

She dug in her heels and stopped right inside the door. "Connor, wait."

Holt turned around and Connor pulled the door shut behind them but stopped walking. Maybe the touch of panic in her voice did it. Connor wasn't sure but whatever it was had him and Holt rushing to give her attention.

She put a hand on Connor's arm and the other on Holt's. "That was him."

"Who?" Holt asked.

"The one on the left." She leaned in, clearly trying to tell them something.

Connor had no idea what. "You lost me."

"On the porch, the taller one." Her words tripped over each other as she raced to get it all out. "He's the man who called you. He was the leader of my kidnapping."

Connor wanted to reassure her and tell her to calm down, but the information had his head spinning. "The blond guy?"

"Good. Nicely done, Jana." Holt grabbed his phone as if he was ready to search the second Connor gave him a name. "Who was it?"

Connor ran through the mental profile he made for the guy. Calling up an image, he tried to make the guy he saw fit in with a former case. Nothing came to him. "I have no idea."

Her head slammed back and her eyes grew wide. "What are you talking about?"

"I've never seen him before. He doesn't register at all." Connor knew that was true. He'd seen awful things but he didn't block memories. If anything, they tended to flood his mind and he had to relive them.

He'd cataloged every case in his head and flipped through them all now.

Again, nothing.

Jana's fingernails dug into his forearm. "That's not possible. He talked as if he knew you."

That didn't make any sense. "I've got a good memory. Not as good as Shane's, but still, it's pretty strong. That guy is not from my past, at least not in any way I remember."

She glanced at Holt before going back to Connor. "That man even knew we were separated."

"We aren't." Connor didn't bother to whisper that time.

She threw up her hands. "Use whatever word you want."

"Married." That was the only word that applied and if someone tried to say something else, especially Marcel, Connor would stop that nonsense and fast.

"You're being difficult."

"Nothing new there," Davis said, his voice breaking in then fading out again.

Holt got their attention when he shifted and reached behind Jana to lock the door. But his attention stayed on Connor. "Let me get this straight—so now people you don't know want you dead?"

"Scary, isn't it?" The news shouldn't have been a surprise. These cases tended to spiderweb and touch everything. This leader could be anyone, maybe even someone Connor didn't know existed until now.

But the answer seemed wrong. The guy who arranged this took a deeply personal angle. Attacking Jana was a direct dig at Connor. It also seemed like something someone with a vendetta would do.

The news still circled Connor's brain but Holt moved

forward. “Seems to me we have two possibilities. Either this guy was a behind-the-scenes type or—”

“Or…” Jana filled in the blank. “He answers to someone else who does know you. Someone we can’t track because we don’t know his identity.”

Davis exhaled and the comm crackled. “More good news.”

“Maybe your friend Drake can help,” Holt said.

“Looks like we have some work to do before he gets here.” At least they had a direction to follow. Connor could remember the two faces he just saw. With him, the team, Jana and Drake, they had a chance at figuring this all out.

But he had a new problem. The third attacker, the guy under the tarp, could be the key. And not seeing that guy’s face made Connor nervous.

Chapter Eleven

Luc drummed his fingers on the steering wheel as he watched Rich jog across the open field toward the waiting sedan. With the car turned off the interior remained deathly quiet, which matched Luc's foul mood. And he wasn't the only one. Bruce sat in the backseat without making a sound as the five-minute waiting mark passed.

After they'd held up under Marcel Lampari's porch they'd made a fast break for the hill behind Marcel's house, but not until Connor and company went inside. The fall back on Plan B was unexpected. So was the lack of return gunfire from inside the house.

None of that explained Rich's notable absence from the operation and the escape.

A warm breeze slipped through the open window and the minutes after sunset cast most of the landscape in darkness. The light Rich carried cut through the night. It moved forward until it blinked out and the front passenger-side door opened.

"I could have predicted that tactical response would fail." Rich shook his head as he slammed the door and stared in the direction he just traveled. "Too wide open. Too unpredictable."

Luc turned on the overhead light and waited for the man to shut up before unloading. "Where were you?"

Rich shrugged. "At the side of the house, as ordered. I sat under that tarp and didn't move. What a waste of time."

He knew full well that wasn't the plan. When Luc and Bruce headed for the porch, Rich should have broken cover and come around the other side. His task was simple: hang back and storm in, taking out the Corcoran men as they stepped outside. But Connor showed up, either without the woman or he had her hidden well enough that Luc didn't see her.

But none of that was the point. "We needed backup and you disappeared."

Rich fiddled with the button for the window. With the car off, each tap produced a click but the window didn't move. "Then your friend here shouldn't have shot my partner. I become risk averse when I don't have someone I trust watching my back."

Luc glanced into the backseat. He expected a reaction from Bruce but the man just sat there. His gun lay on the seat next to him but he didn't reach for it.

"You want to help me here?" Luc asked him.

"Rich knows he messed up." Bruce stared at the other man, daring him to deny it. "He was trying to prove a point. Now that he's taken his stand he'll conform. Correct?"

Rich's eyes narrowed. "I didn't—"

"But you're both missing the point." Bruce brushed something off his dark shirt. Something it seemed only he could see. "There is a bright spot in all of this."

Luc shook his head. "Not that I can see."

"Which is?" Rich asked at the same time.

"We have a number and we know faces." Bruce delivered the comment then stopped. When the other men stared without saying a word, he continued. "In addition to Lampari we have three from this Corcoran team staked out in the house and the woman, who had to be there somewhere. There's no way a man like Connor Bowen would dump her somewhere unless he has access to a bunker, and I doubt that."

The replay only made Luc's anger rise. "We should have been able to handle that number of men and subdue Connor. This could be over."

It qualified as a missed opportunity in Luc's view. The boss expected results. Failure was not an option. If that meant taking out Rich like Bruce had with Reno, Luc would do it.

There was no way he was paying for this mess. He already had a scapegoat. That plan needed one step, one word from him, and it would be in motion.

"While it's not easy to collect information on the Corcoran Team, my intel says there are more players," Bruce said, talking as if Luc had never spoken. "We may have gotten lucky dealing with only three."

Rich laughed. "One or two more. I still like those odds."

As if Luc needed further proof that hiring Rich had been a major misstep. The man worked on his own schedule and the results frequently turned out sloppy. He didn't reason anything through.

The only way to end his position was with a bullet, but Luc needed him right now. "If you think the odds are even, you haven't been paying attention."

Rich wedged his body into the corner and leaned against the door. "Meaning?"

This part should be obvious, even to Rich and his muddled brain. "Look at the body count. There's not even a paper cut on Connor's side."

For about the hundredth time since this operation started Luc regretted not taking a knife to Jana when he had the chance. Injuring her, making her bleed or at least injuring her so she was unable to run would have made the tracking easier. Would have slowed her down and increased Connor's vulnerability.

This is what happened when he decided to be nice. The last time Luc made that mistake he had to double back and clean up his mess. Let it slide when a kid snuck in and saw a transfer that wasn't supposed to be happening and you ended up with a potentially chatty witness. Scare the crap out of him, threaten to take out his family in the nastiest way possible, then agree not to follow through when the kid begged and you took a big risk. Find out he ran home and told his father and then the whole family had to die.

But that's what fire was for. Luc didn't make the rules. He just followed them.

That's where it all started. The boss kept his fingerprints out of the official records and helped the evidence disappear. Someone else went to prison for the family massacre and ever since, Luc had a debt to repay. Connor would serve as the final payment.

Rich turned in his seat and faced Bruce. "What's the next step?"

The subtle shift in power bothered Luc. This was his operation. Bruce stepping in and giving orders confused the division of labor. Also threatened to make Luc irrelevant, and that couldn't happen. Not when Bruce had been handpicked by the boss and his reports could say anything.

Luc jumped in. He had to bring the attention back to him before the leadership role slipped away from him. "Same as it's always been. Grab Jana and if we can get Connor, take him, as well. Otherwise, she's a lure to catch him."

Rich scoffed. "I still don't get why we can't just blow up the house."

Luc did like fire, but not this time. "The boss wants

Connor alive but messed up over his missing wife. One mistake with fire and we lose everything."

"This is the same boss I'm not allowed to meet."

"Exactly." Luc refused to have this argument again. You'd think the man would learn since the last round ended with his friend getting a bullet in the brain.

"We go in tonight." Bruce's bored tone suggested the entire conversation amounted to a waste of his time. "Wait until they're comfortable and feeling attack-proof in the bunkhouse where she's been staying. Clearly she's back there now."

"Let's storm the place now. Shoot first and collect our money."

That appeared to be Rich's answer for everything. No wonder the military gave him a one-way ticket out well before his service should have been up. He was too volatile. Too wild for Luc's taste.

"A little finesse is needed," Bruce explained. "We have dead bodies strewn all across the desert. Someone is going to notice soon."

Luc knew their troubles reached beyond the dead. The desert would clean up some of that mess for them. Animals and weather would cover tracks and drag bones.

Shutting down a charity that should be up and running was a different story. "And sooner or later someone is going to want to get in touch with the charity and not be able to get a person, and we'll have a mess. All it takes is one nosy sort to get the ball rolling before we can finish the job."

Bruce picked up his gun and placed it on his lap. "We slip in tonight and take her out of her bed in the bunkhouse, like I wanted to originally instead of grabbing her at the office."

Wrong answer. Now Bruce appeared as clueless as the

idiot next to Luc in the front seat. "I'm pretty sure we'll be tripping over Connor if we do."

"What happened to them being separated?" Rich asked.

Bruce shrugged. It was one of the few moves he made since he sat down. "Looks like someone forgot to tell Connor."

Which was why they needed a clearer plan. Preferably one that involved a quick snatch. Luc used some common sense to put the brakes on the odd bromance blooming in the car. "So we wait."

"No." Bruce picked up his gun. "We go in at three."

Rich clapped his hands. "And now we have a plan."

TWO HOURS LATER, night settled in and so did Jana. She'd showered in the space she'd used as her temporary Utah home while Connor and Holt talked strategy outside. Then Connor disappeared over to Marcel's house and Cam took over what she guessed was the equivalent of wife guard duty.

She wanted to have a clue as to what passed between Connor and Marcel. Knowing Connor's mood, she assumed it wasn't good. He'd been furious that the gunfire followed them to the house. Jana got him out of the family room before he abandoned his control. She had to because Connor's team seemed fine with letting him tear Marcel apart.

That was her fault. She'd stoked the jealousy without meaning to. The decision made sense in her head, or it had at the time. Other than the house with Connor, she didn't have a home base or an old family homestead like most people did. Her father had moved them around, which kept her relationship roots shallow.

Looking now, the poor judgment behind her Utah choice hit her and she slumped down on the temporary bed she'd been using for months. She suddenly hated the one-room apartment. It stood for everything she'd done wrong.

She'd acted impulsively and now dealt with bouts of regret. She felt naive and stupid. Finding space, running to Utah instead of any other place, only widened the gap between her and Connor. They loved each other and talked about Marcel and work issues, but they never moved one step closer to a solution.

Wearing one of Connor's faded T-shirts—her favorite one—and a pair of oversized boxer shorts, she crossed her legs and stared at the closed bathroom door. Maybe it just seemed as if Connor was taking the longest shower in history. After all, he wasn't exactly the run-from-adversity type.

The second she thought it the door pushed open. Steam rolled out and the smell of soap washed over her. Connor stepped out wearing boxerbriefs and nothing else. It was as if he wanted to test her.

The long muscular legs and flat stomach. The tanned chest and scruff of hair over his chin. From the wet, black hair to the shiny gold wedding band on his finger he was the most attractive man she'd ever met. So sexy he made something in her stomach flutter.

From the beginning, he overwhelmed her senses. Back then he'd been careful not to further injure her already broken arm. He kept up a steady line of conversation, nonsense stuff mostly, but his voice hypnotized her. Even now she'd sit and listen to him talk to the team or on the phone and get a little breathless. Firm, husky and so confident.

Her father would have liked him. Any mother would adore him. He was the kind of man who would keep his woman safe.

If only she could just teach him to loosen his hold.

He dried his hair with a towel then dropped it on the floor. Just like home. "What is this place?"

"A sort of bunkhouse." She scooted over to make room when he looked like he intended to sit next to her rather than in one of the two oversized chairs in the small sitting area of the room. "We get volunteers and workers come in from the field. Marcel built and maintains this space for them to cut down on administrative costs. There are two apartments like this and then a regular bunkhouse."

"Holt and Shane are setting up in there. I heard Shane call the top bunk." Connor folded his hands on his lap as his thigh rested against hers. "They'll take turns keeping watch until Drake arrives."

"Will that be soon?"

"He lives in Oregon and happened to be home instead of out on assignment."

"With?"

"The group I used to work for. He's on the way over and should arrive any time. Davis is guiding him in."

She didn't pry because the name didn't matter. She knew what the rough work did to Connor, how it hardened his edges and shuttered his emotions, and wondered if she'd see the same reflected in Drake. "Poor Davis should get some rest. He has a baby on the way."

"Not sleeping will be good practice for after the birth." Connor's gaze roamed before landing on the table. The same table where she's set up two of their couple photos. "You've been staying here."

She seriously considered punching him in the shoulder. Not hard, but enough to prove her point. "Of course. Where did you think I'd been sleeping?"

He shot her the side eye. "You don't want to know."

Not a surprise but her temper spiked. Zoomed right off the scale.

She turned to face him. “Connor, you can’t think—” When he picked up her hand and caressed each finger, her voice cut off.

“When you’re desperate and angry your mind spins. I can apologize for it if you need that, but it’s not as if I wanted to believe you left me for him.”

She squeezed his hand and stared at him, not saying a word, until he looked up and gave her eye contact again. “I left you because you spent so much time planning my protection that we stopped living.”

“That’s not true.”

“You wanted me to wear a tracker while I was out of the house.” And that was just the start of his odd behavior. It escalated until anxiety ran wild inside her. Without a crackdown in her exaggerated state she feared he’d take her keys and trap her indoors.

“It’s not like the one criminals wear.”

The idea he thought that was the line started a steady banging in her head. “Is that the point?”

“I actually have no idea, since you wearing it doesn’t seem weird to me.”

She guessed she had to spell it out. “It was a tag.”

“Yeah, so?”

In her mind his response proved her point. “Doesn’t that strike you as overkill?”

He dragged her hand to his lap. “I deal in danger. Part of my job is to anticipate problems and neutralize them.”

“You just used the word neutralize in connection with your wife.”

“Not neutralize you. I meant…” The corner of his mouth lifted. “Okay, I can see where my word choice was a tad clinical.”

Yeah, if he smiled and agreed with her and sat there looking all delicious they’d never make any progress.

Being on the mattress this close and smelling his familiar scent already wore her down. Much more of that thing where he skimmed his finger over her bare skin and all those months of being apart would back up on her. She missed touching him. The intimacy.

But this was too important to gloss over and let him write off as a poor word choice. "I asked you to ease up on the boundaries and in response you ran a background check on a woman I met in my exercise class."

"She introduced herself to you."

"To borrow a towel."

"Look, a check in that circumstance is not that unusual for someone in my line of work. Even Joel backed me up on that. He's the one who ran the check, not me."

The man could be a lawyer with those arguing skills. "You asked him to, and since he works for you he did it without question, so don't try to sell the innocent act."

Connor hummed. "Well, yeah. I guess that's true."

That was the man she knew and loved. The same one who thought this sort of thing made sense. "Then you had Joel follow her."

"Only once." Connor held up a finger as if that made everything better.

She refused to fight over the number of times since that wasn't the point, as he well knew. "It was creepy."

"I don't want you hurt."

"And I want balance."

He lifted their joined hands and kissed each of her knuckles. "You could have just said that."

"I did. Many times." Her voice bobbled as a shiver ran through her. "You nodded and agreed and then hid a GPS in my wallet without telling me."

He trapped her hand against his chest. With the smallest

of movements he pulled her in closer to his side. "Davis told me I'd pay for that one."

"He's a smart man."

"He's not so lax with safety now that he's married." Connor's hand went to her hair and he slipped the strands through his fingers as his gaze traveled over her face. "Do you understand my fear for you?"

"You tackled me to outrun a bullet yesterday.... Wait, was that only yesterday?" She shook her head to clear out the thought. "Point is, I'm not convinced you're afraid of anything."

One minute she sat on the mattress and the next she curled up on his lap. He lifted her, moved her and she was so mesmerized by the combination of his words and touches that she didn't notice until her butt balanced against his thighs.

One arm wrapped around her back and the other settled over her hand on her belly. "The only thing in this world I fear, the one thing guaranteed to rob my sleep and drop me to my knees in panic when you're not looking, is the thought of losing you."

Her heart did a little flip. Actually felt as if it spun around and landed hard. "Connor."

"But I pushed you away." His nose went to her hair and he nuzzled her ear. "I hate that you felt you needed to run from me."

She couldn't let him take that on. For weeks, maybe even months she did blame him for not getting a clue. But as the days dragged on she faced up a very real failing of her own. She didn't stop and fight harder. "I'm the one who ran away."

"Yes."

She pulled back until he lifted his head and looked at her. She searched his eyes looking for the answer and when she found it, she said it out loud. "You're angry with me about that."

It wasn't a question. She said it as a statement because she needed him to admit it. He spent a lot of time burying feelings and one thing he never did was place blame on her. This time, certainly during the last few phone calls, he went from general conversation to anger. She hoped it was a sign of some sort.

He shook his head. "I get it."

"You don't."

"It doesn't—"

"Connor, come on. Say it. You're angry. There's a part of you that feels betrayed. I hate that because I never meant to do that to you, but you have a right to your feelings."

His mouth opened and closed. Finally the breath ran out of him and his shoulders fell. "Do you blame me for being frustrated and more than a little confused?"

She closed her eyes, grateful that he finally vented, if only a fraction of what she guessed rumbled around inside him. "That's what I'm saying. No, I don't. It's normal and human and, honestly, it gives me hope."

He blinked and as fast as the tension rose, it all vanished. Confusion took its place. "You actually want me to be furious with you?"

"I want you to care. To be invested enough to be honest."

"Then you should be thrilled because I do care. I love you with every part of me." He shifted her until her knees straddled his hips and she faced him. "More than I thought possible. More than I have with any other person ever."

The intimate position had her thinking about anything but fighting. Probably had something to do with the bulge growing under her and the way his fingers trailed up her bare back. "I thought we were talking."

"You promised me a seduction."

Her shirt started to lift. In a few more inches the bottom would be at her shoulders. "We're not done."

"That's exactly what I've been saying anytime anyone suggests we're separated."

Her fingers slipped through his damp hair. "Well, technically I meant the discussion just then."

"Let me show you how together we are."

His mouth covered hers and words began to spin in her brain. She couldn't form a sentence or count to ten. All she knew was the heat radiating off him and the touch of his fingers as he cupped her breasts under the edge of her shirt.

The kiss lingered and enticed. His lips worked their magic as his tongue slipped inside her mouth. He was under her and around her. His need pulsed through her. Time fell away and their problems melted. This was about their bodies and their need for each other.

She got lost in the kiss and didn't notice he'd stripped off her shirt and lowered her to the bed until her bare back slid against the comforter. The kisses traveled down her neck. Gentle sucking and the rough scrape of this tongue—she loved it all.

Her knees rose until her feet fell flat against the mattress. She pressed her thighs tight against his hips and felt a shudder run through him.

When he lifted up on his elbows and balanced his upper body over her, she ran a hand over his chest. She loved the feel of him, so strong and yet so gentle with her. Except when he wasn't and she begged him to keep going. She loved that part, too.

"It's been so long." She kissed his mouth then his neck.

"Forever."

He slipped out of her hold and moved down her body. His lips found her breasts and teased. Back and forth, his tongue swept over her until her hips lifted off the bed. A kiss and a nip and her nerve endings tingled.

He kissed, licking his tongue over her nipples, one after the other, until they formed hard peaks, while one hand slid under the elastic band of her shorts. The other caressed her breasts then moved to her stomach.

He treated every inch of her to a barrage of sensations. Unable to lie still, she kicked her legs and tried to push him lower. She wanted his mouth on her and those shorts off.

He rose up, kneeling between her upraised thighs. Fingertips trailed over her skin and he never broke contact. The shorts slipped off and landed on the floor. The panties went next.

When she looked down again she saw her bare body and his dark hair. Felt his tongue flick against her. Pleasure crashed over her as thoughts bombarded her brain. Him inside her. Him holding her. She wanted it all.

"Are you still on the pill?" His fingers pushed inside her.

Her head fell back against the bed. "Yes."

His body stilled for the briefest of seconds then his hands went to work again. "Good."

"For you." She plowed her fingers through his hair and lifted his head just far enough to see his eyes. "I wanted to be ready for when I came home to you."

"I've waited forever to hear that."

Heat surged and his thumb brushed against her. Pressure built and her body caught fire until all she wanted was to drag him up and pull him in closer. "Connor, please."

Still, he didn't give in. He continued to touch her, lick her. Place soft kisses on her inner thighs. He kept up the sensual torture until her muscles shook and she drew in large gasps of air in an effort to breathe. Her legs dropped open wider and her chest rose and fell. Sensations she hadn't felt and desperately missed overtook her until she chanted his name.

When she opened her eyes again, ready and so primed she thought anything could set her off, he hovered over her. His mouth fused with hers as he entered her. Being so tightly wound, the feel of him had her head falling back and her body clenching around him. She didn't know when he took the briefs off or how she missed the pleasure of stripping them down, but the friction had her back arching and her fingernails digging into his shoulders.

"Yes." The word punched out of her on a hard breath.

He slapped a hand on the mattress beside her head and clenched the comforter in his fist. The bed rocked and his body pushed and pulled inside her until the blood left her head. Then his finger brushed against the very heat of her, right on that spot that made everything inside her uncoil.

When the orgasm stormed through her, her muscles tightened and her mouth went wild. Kissing him. Tasting him. Tension pinned her to the bed, squeezed the life out of her and had her panting.

Just as her muscles loosened he stiffened above her. A second later his shoulders shook and his chest dipped closer to hers. With his face buried in her neck, his body pumping against her, he breathed in deep and blew air across her skin. His body bucked and his head dropped even farther. One last sharp exhale and his elbows gave out.

When the shaking passed, his weight fell against her. For a few minutes she lay there. The quiet blanketed them and their breathing returned to normal. She should roll him to the side. Maybe say something smart. Aim for charming. Instead, she trailed her fingers over his shoulders, loving the feel of him.

Her last thought before she drifted off was of him. Of them. Of how they had to make it work.

Chapter Twelve

An hour later Connor found jeans and a tee and stepped out onto the porch of Jana's temporary housing. After the amazing session in bed his muscles had turned to mush. He was half surprised he could walk.

Being inside her felt so right but had wiped out most of his energy. He hoped the cool night air would revive him. Seeing the stars uncorrupted by city lights and heavy clouds usually helped. No way could he afford to drift off. His men might have guard duty, but he intended to be ready for anything.

Shame nothing prepared him for his own wife. During sex and during the quiet times everything about her worked for him. One look, the right word, and all those years of refining his control turned to waste.

As she ran through his litany of protective measures earlier, he had to fight off a wince. Admittedly, all lined up like that, the list sounded crazy. The individual pieces made sense at the time, at least in his head. He laid them out and she balked. He handled her objections and assumed they were okay. He thought everything ended up fine. That she understood. In reality, she plotted her escape.

Maybe he had become crazed and over the top. But the kidnapping proved that when he let up, she got hurt.

He rubbed his head as he tried to work it through. The soft whistle had him turning. "Hey."

Holt moved under the porch light. Even in the darkness, the smirk was tough to miss. "You're up early."

Connor decided to ignore the amusement. "Want me to take a shift?" He secretly hoped he'd say no.

Holt shrugged as he swallowed a smile. "I figured you'd be too busy to work."

Temptation lingered but Connor decided not to kick his friend's sorry butt. Truth was Connor had been busy and would be again as soon as he could wake Jana up without feeling guilty about it.

He'd dug down deep and found control he didn't know he possessed. Months apart only fed his need for her. That whole absence making the heart do…whatever…turned out to be true. Without her, the days dragged and the nights proved unbearable.

Still, there were rules, and not talking with the boys about sex with the wife had to be one of them. "I'm thinking Jana would kill me if I agreed to that or said anything about what happened behind that closed door."

This time Holt laughed, drowning out the noises of the desert. "I know you must be spending at least part of your time begging her to come back."

Connor moved out to the end of the porch after checking the door behind him. He leaned on the post and stood up again when it groaned under his weight. Sand and rock littered the ground around them but he couldn't see much of anything. For some reason that struck him as wrong but he didn't analyze it.

The begging thing. No question he had some groveling ahead of him. There was no need to fight it or pretend his future didn't include that. "Yeah, well, I'm about to turn on the charm and start pleading."

Holt stopped smoothing his heel over a loose floorboard and looked at Connor. "You could have told us, you know."

"About what?"

"That she left." Holt's gaze didn't waver and the intensity suggested the conversation meant something to him. "You handed us a lot of lines and false stories about where she was and when she was coming back. You held it in."

"There was nothing any of you could do."

"We could have bought you a beer or taken you for crabs." Holt looked like he wanted to throw his body off a cliff. "Figure out how to listen, or whatever it is women talk about wanting."

"I didn't know what to do, Holt. I really didn't." Connor wanted to shirk the conversation off. Crack and joke and act like it didn't matter. But it did.

"And then you lied to us. I don't think you've ever lied to us about anything else. We kind of depend on that."

"The choice was wrong. Way wrong and I'm sorry for it." The nibbling guilt bit harder. "It's just that the looks on your faces…"

"Because we care about you. About her."

Talking emotions and private matters didn't come easy to Connor. Living where he worked tied everything together but he tried to separate out what he could. But in the end these men were his friends and he lied to them by omission, and on occasion outright when he made up excuses for her absence. They deserved better.

Not knowing how to explain it, Connor went with a sensation he thought Holt would understand. "I'm not really into pity. I couldn't figure out how to lead while sounding so pathetic over losing her."

"You're overthinking. It's likely we would have put you on a plane with Cam and made you come out here to fetch your wife." Holt closed one eye. "Man, you should have stopped this nonsense long before now."

Connor felt his defenses rise. There were only two people in the marriage and no one else could understand. But he appreciated Holt wanting Jana home. It was hard to argue with that sentiment since Connor craved the same thing.

"She wasn't ready to come back." He took the next step and said the words that crushed him. "I'm not sure if she is now."

Holt rested his hands on the gun slung over his shoulder. "Nah, the woman I saw loves her husband."

Connor knew that much. He saw it in every movement and every smile. "Believe it or not, that might not be enough to weather this."

After blowing out a labored breath, Holt joined Connor at the edge of the porch. They both stared out over the dark night but Holt was the first to talk. "I don't know anything about marriage."

"Or women."

Holt snorted. "Probably true. Honestly, I'm afraid to check in at the Annapolis office lately because relationship fever seems to be sweeping the place. It's like a virus or something."

The idea of this strong man—the one with shoulders that suggested he could lift a building and eat a sandwich at the same time—running scared from romance made Connor smile. He got it.

He once said things like that. Then the right woman stepped into his life and he stopped saying uninformed things. "Such a romantic."

"And now Davis is going to be a dad."

Connor still couldn't adjust to that. Davis was rock solid. He followed Connor's lead and kept the team in order. The thought of him holding this tiny person refused to register in Connor's head. But he knew Davis would be great at it. He'd been handed a pretty terrible upbringing. No way would he inflict the same on his kid. Those differences resulted in team changes.

The fact Davis changed his priorities said it all to Connor. "He'll be a good one."

"No doubt, but I don't want any part of any of that."

The bachelors in the group were downright crazed when they said things like this. The entire traveling team got wide eyed and twitchy at the mention of women.

Connor had seen it all before. "Funny, but I'm pretty sure I once heard Davis say the same thing. Davis and Joel and Pax and—"

"Like I said, a virus. Make that a plague."

Connor chuckled at the way Holt ran scared. "Nice."

"But, honestly, we've known each other a long time."

Conversations that started that way generally ran downhill. Connor braced for impact. "True."

"There's no way she's with Marcel."

The sentence bounced around in Connor's head. Through the waves of jealousy he'd come to the same conclusion. "I know."

Holt grunted. "Huh, that turned out easier than I expected. Thought I'd have to convince you, maybe threaten to beat you."

Last thing he needed was a hit to the head from this guy. "I'm slow, not stupid."

"I'm not sure I'd agree with that," came a voice from the darkness.

Holt's gun came up and he shifted into position. The barrel aimed into a dark patch at the back of Marcel's house. Connor considered it a blind spot, but they were not under attack. He recognized that voice.

He tapped his hand against Holt's gun. "Ease up."

A figure broke through the shadows and stood on the edge of the circle of light. Blond and forty, he was a few years older than Connor and probably more fit thanks to his current black ops position. He'd served as a mentor and represented most of Connor's good memories of the group who used to employ him.

Holt took in the other man and slowly lowered his weapon. "Drake, I'm guessing."

"And you're…let me guess." Drake snapped his fingers as he thought it through. "Holt?"

Holt nodded and held out a hand. "Impressive."

"Wish I could take the credit for being so astute, but Davis sent photos for me to study during the plane ride. Something about making sure I didn't shoot a member of the team."

"Sounds like him." Connor could always count on Davis.

Drake frowned. "Speaking of which, I lost my cell coverage. Looks like there's a block around here."

Connor didn't like going blind. "Davis and the rest of the team are working on that."

With the welcomes and general information behind them, Connor concentrated on the man he once knew. He was more slender but still possessed a laser-like focus that increased his already off-the-charts intensity.

"How are you?" A handshake turned into a quick hug complete with back slapping.

"Better than you." When Drake backed away one of his eyebrows lifted. "Is it true you let Jana get away?"

Apparently the state of his marriage had made the news. Connor shuddered at the thought. "Only temporarily."

"I still say if I had been the one to move in for the rescue rather than taking lookout, she'd be married to me and you'd be living in a trailer somewhere with a cat."

Holt barked out a laugh. "Interesting choices."

"She hasn't seen you in years, so she might still pick you." That was the fear. Connor worried that because of his fumbling and heavy-handed protection tactics she'd pick anyone but him.

"Right." Drake tucked his fingers in back pockets and rocked back on his heels. "So what do we have here?"

"Messed up charity shipments, someone who wants me dead and a kidnapping." Connor ticked off the list, knowing which line items Drake would hook on to.

"So, the usual," Holt mumbled.

"Charity as in Boundless?" Drake glared at Connor.

"Yep."

"You used to swear Marcel was dirty, that his story was off." Drake joined them in kicking stones. "I figured your radar was off because he wanted your woman."

"Even then?" Holt asked.

Connor didn't know why it was a surprise since he didn't exactly hide the ongoing Marcel issue. "Told you."

"Marcel's not her type. She likes big and dumb." Drake slapped Connor on the back as he made the joke.

"Thanks."

Drake stared at Marcel's house. "I say we pick the charity apart until we find something."

Holt raised a hand. "I'm in."

This is exactly what Connor thought would happen. Drake assessed and planned. He stepped in and immediately started to plot out a retrieval plan. This time wasn't any different.

They needed the extra manpower. And no matter how tough Cam was, the guy could use a break and someone other than Davis to talk to, if he could even do that with all the communication problems on this job. "I have a man over there."

"Enough said." Drake straightened his belt buckle. "Tell him I'm on the way."

Connor watched his friend disappear again. It's what he did. Move in, clean up, vanish. It was the unofficial motto of his old office. Having Drake here dulled the edges of Connor's tension. Maybe he could settle down and enjoy a few more minutes with his wife without worrying who could sneak up behind him.

He was about to go back inside when Holt's voice stopped him. "Notice the darkness."

Connor stared out over the shapes that looked like blobs. "That happens at night."

Shifting his feet and moving in a slow one-eighty, Holt pointed at the roof lines of the buildings. "I mean it's too dark. Looks like someone turned off the sensor lights."

"Interesting." And like that, Connor's tension came zooming back. It filled his body and choked off the air around him. The tick in the back of his neck returned as well. "Any chance they were broken by the guys from the porch?"

"No glass."

Because, of course, he had already checked. Holt was like that. Connor knew because he refined the other man's training. Not that it took much since Holt bordered on fighting machine when he threw in with Corcoran.

"Footprints?" Connor asked.

Holt shook his head. "No signs of tampering from the outside."

The words he didn't say made all the difference. Without cut wires or any other evidence of vandalism, the options dwindled. He loved when that happened. Knowing the players was essential and right now he guessed at their identities. Factoring out his personal feelings wasn't always easy but the possibilities did keep dwindling.

"So, we're talking turned off from inside the house." And since Connor knew his team didn't cause the damage, the suspect pool shrank again.

"Possible."

Which Connor took to mean definitely.

From the beginning he'd been looking and assuming the danger rose out of something he'd done. With the repeated attacks and news of the inventory inconsistencies, his view had changed. The anger the leader attached to him. There was more than a twinge of something personal and nasty going on. Connor got that.

There was no question Jana's role here was as a pawn. She served as the fastest road to him. But he couldn't separate out his work from the charity. He knew there was a link but couldn't quite get a handle on it.

"I hate Marcel." He did. Right down to his bones. Hated his look and his voice and really despised the way he looked at Jana.

In certain circles he was viewed as a savior. Connor looked and saw a phony. Jana had been in his care as an employee of sorts twice and got kidnapped both times. Either she'd found something or her conscience served as a potential burden. Something wasn't right and it all traced back to Marcel. It had to.

"Sounds like your dislike is not without reason. Frankly, I'm amazed you can get through ten minutes without punching that guy," Holt said with a trace of anger in his voice. "Do we confront him now?"

Connor thought the punching part sounded good. Shut down the charity and throw the guy in jail. Connor knew it wasn't rational and the evidence he had didn't support any of it, but in this case reason flew out the window.

Maybe Jana was right and he did have a problem with overkill.

Rather than moving in too fast, Connor went for smart. "Not yet."

"You want more evidence?"

They needed something other than a few inventory slips. Marcel would pass the blame to a young staffer or overzealous employee overseas, just like he did before. "I want him to lead us straight into whatever mess he's made. Catch him in the act."

"I'm thinking we won't have to wait long."

Connor hoped that was true because he had much better things to do with his nights. "Be ready."

Chapter Thirteen

Hidden next to a ridge behind Marcel's property, they waited. Luc shook his head as the newest kidnaping plan blew up around him. Not that he minded since he thought the whole thing suffered from too much ego and too little thought. Still, getting outmaneuvered by Connor ticked him off.

Rich jumped off the hood of the truck and grabbed the binoculars out of Luc's hands. "Who is that?"

Rich looked, even leaned in. Bruce didn't say a word.

Thanks to the poor lighting and bad angle, Luc couldn't make out the face of the newcomer down there on the porch. He saw the cocky walk and the comfortable conversation with Connor. Since the guy didn't get shot, Luc had to assume the Corcoran folks considered him safe.

That was not good news. Down so many men, Luc didn't need more targets. "Another player."

Keys jangled as Bruce shoved them back in his pocket. "We need to hang back. Come at this from a different angle. Maybe wait until daylight so we can see who's moving around down there."

Rich's hand dropped and he slammed the expensive equipment against the truck's hood. "That wasn't the plan. I want the rest of my money and to get out of here, and that means finishing this."

Since he never sanctioned this idea, Luc wasn't married to completing it now. He refrained from pointing out he never thought this was a good idea. "We need a new plan."

Grabbing the woman got harder the more men Connor had on his side. And now everyone appeared to be awake and walking around. That stole their advantage. Made getting in and out and catching Connor literally with his pants down impossible.

"Do you recognize the newest guy?" Bruce asked Luc.

"Not from here, but his presence changes things."

Bruce nodded but Rich looked back and forth between the other men, his face reddening as he watched the byplay. "Why?"

Luc didn't think Rich could get more clueless. Turned out he was wrong. "We could be dealing with more of Connor's men or outside law enforcement. There are too many variables we don't know."

"New plan." Bruce headed for the driver's door. "We get closer then head off on foot. We'll sneak into Marcel's house and do a little recon."

Rich frowned. "I thought there was someone on guard in there and we had to pull back or whatever else you two have been saying. What happened to all the warnings from two seconds ago?"

"Connor is with his wife. The big one is walking the property and the other one went into the bunkhouse." Rich ran through the list and mentally double-checked it to make sure he hadn't missed anything obvious. "We have a lot of awake people but one who might not be."

The confusion hadn't cleared from Rich's face. "And the new guy?"

Luc reached around Rich and picked up his binoculars. Adjusting the lenses, he scanned the area and stopped when he spied a lone figure walking in the darkness and ducking into a car. "Looks like he's leaving for now."

"Okay then, let's grab the woman."

"No." Luc grew tired of giving that answer.

Rich clicked his tongue against the back of his teeth. "So what's in the house you two think is so important?"

Luc didn't need Bruce's help. That one was easy. "Answers."

JANA WOKE UP when Connor crawled back into bed. Technically, she'd been asleep since he closed the door behind him and went outside.

It had always been that way. He moved or shifted and she came awake with a start. Something about not having him at her side made her jumpy.

The months apart had been sleepless and frustrating. Holding him, making love with him tonight, made her realize she'd given up way more than the simple joys of marriage. Talking to him across a table, discussing something one of the men had said…touching him.

He snuggled in behind her and wrapped an arm around her stomach. His fingers went searching a second later.

She stopped the wandering by putting a hand over his. "What time is it?"

"Late, or maybe I should say early." His mouth found her throat and he kissed a line down her neck.

The words vibrated against her sensitive skin. "What were you doing?"

His tongue trailed along her shoulder. "Talking to Drake."

Leave it to Connor to name drop while his hands made a move on her breasts. Nice try.

She turned over onto her back and stared up at Connor. The small light on the other side of the room gave the bedroom area a soft glow. The lighting only highlighted his dark good looks. Staring up at the man she loved so much, she forgot what she was going to say.

His mouth kicked up in a sexy grin. "Yes?"

"What?" But he got it. That knowing look said he understood what he did to her and was happy to use that as a weapon to get his way.

"Yes, Drake is here," Connor said, filling in her mental blanks. "He's going over to cover Cam and check out the charity office."

"Am I ever going to meet this man? I've seen emails and photos and heard your side of telephone conversations." Drake meant something to Connor and therefore to her.

Her husband wasn't the bring-friends-home type. He hung out with his team. They bonded and supported each other. Worked hard and got together to watch football and do whatever it was that had them laughing downstairs at the house.

But Drake held a piece of Connor's past. They'd depended on each other through what she gathered were tough days filled with danger and death. That kind of thing had to imprint on both of them.

She often thought Connor limited his contact with Drake in order to limit the reminders of all they'd seen. She understood. Well, as much as she could as someone who fought death through other means. Still, she wanted to meet the man who meant so much to Connor. Thank him for getting her husband through the tough times.

And maybe Drake could give her a hint about how to handle Connor and his demons.

Right now he trailed his fingers over her collarbone, brushing and teasing. "Drake is not exactly a guy who brings a bottle of wine and sits down at dinner to chat."

Connor had been the same way when they met. She

insisted on dates and dinners and some sense of normalcy. For her, he made the adjustments. "I'm sure your friend eats."

"Let me put it this way—if you considered me feral when we got married…"

"That's an overstatement, but yes." Her hand went to his hair. She loved the feel of the strands through her fingers. She'd missed so much about him and about being with him, but that easy pleasure ranked pretty high on the list.

"I am full-on domesticated compared to Drake. He's been in the field since he graduated from college." Connor lowered his head and dropped a kiss on the top of her breast. "He stalks and hides and fixes."

"And kills." She waited for Connor to freeze.

He kept kissing and caressing, moving lower until his mouth hovered over her breast. "More than you would think and not always for sound reasons. He followed the orders when I no longer could."

The strangeness of the conversation—the topics so hard and rough—while Connor whipped her body into a frenzy and made her want to crawl all over him summed up their relationship. From the beginning they'd mixed the danger with the pleasure. She guessed that part of their lives counted as pretty abnormal.

A thought struck her. "Do you not want me to meet him?"

"Honestly, I thought you already did. Way back, I mean. We talk about you all the time and he speaks as if he knows you, which I guess he does in a way. The version of you he hears from me."

She felt him smile against her skin. "That sounds bad."

"The exact opposite, actually."

"That's good to know."

"But the fact we don't hang out with him is not about

hiding you or protecting you from his rough side." Connor pushed up on his elbow again and stared down at her. "It's really about him never standing still long enough to hold him down for anything."

"We all seem to be trapped here until we figure this out, and that includes him." It felt right to finally meet the mysterious man behind the cryptic description.

"Yes, it does."

"He won't be able to run from me."

Connor rolled into her until his erection brushed her thigh. Before she could catch his mouth for a kiss, he started moving. Down he went, stopping only to nuzzle her in all the right places.

He rubbed his head back and forth against her stomach until the rough stubble had her body begging for more. One hot kiss against her skin and her stomach dipped. Then he did it again.

"I can't imagine any man wanting to get away from you." He traveled even lower.

Her fingers slipped over his head, guiding him to where she wanted him and then holding him in place. "So sweet."

"Actually, I thought I'd show you how dirty I can be."

Chapter Fourteen

They snuck in using the same entrance they'd escaped from before. The outside sensor lights didn't click on. The video monitors had been purchased but not installed. The alarm system took care of the outside gate and the doors. Move a window and a wailing noise would blast through the still house. But they weren't using a regular entrance.

Crouched down and quiet, they'd moved across the property, heading in from the ridge. It was the one blind spot in the yard. A slim patch of land between the shed and the house. No lights. No warnings.

The latch under the porch gave without trouble. On their stomachs and shuffling in, they moved one by one until they reached the open area about three feet high where they could push up. Lifting the floorboard into the back office proved harder. With his palms flat against the outline of the trap door, Luc shoved but something heavy weighed it down.

Luc motioned to Bruce and Rich to wait. No knowing how or what lurked on the other side required them to be even more careful. He didn't trust either of the other men to do the job. No, he would take on this task without them. Bruce could pretend to lead another time. Rich could whine on someone else's dime.

Luc tried again. When Bruce reached over and added

his strength, the door gave with a soft click. Luc waited for shots to fire through, for footsteps or something. When the room above stayed quiet, he decided to move. Leaving the other men squatting in the dirt, Luc threw more of his energy into the task and the door lifted about a foot.

He slipped his hand through the opening and felt something soft. A rug of some sort. Figured on this job something mundane and stupid would almost sidetrack him. He made a space wide enough to shimmy through then lowered the door again. The small thud echoed but he knew it would blend into the noise of the desert.

With his gun in his hand, he took careful steps across the room to the hallway. A light burned at the end where the kitchen and family room area stood. Luc heard shuffling and the clinking of glasses. The person out there was either the one Corcoran man assigned to the house or Marcel.

Luc slid along the hall. He got close to the end and saw the flash of an elbow as the man in there moved around. Luc took in the hiking boots and dark pants. Nothing about this guy's form resembled Marcel's slim look. This had to be the trained killer.

Knowing that had Luc moving back down the hall to the bedroom. Slow and even steps that kept the wood beneath him from creaking. The bedroom door was closed. Luc turned the knob gradually to eliminate any noise. Since it wasn't locked, it pushed open in his hand.

Slipping inside he saw the lump in the bed and the kitchen knife on the nightstand. Luc had to give the guy credit for being prepared. Too bad it wasn't enough. Bullets beat blades every single time.

As Luc got to the side of the bed near the weapon, the lump moved. Marcel flipped to his back and his eyes popped open. Luc had his hand over his mouth before he could yell.

After a second, Marcel shoved the hand away and pushed up on his elbows. "It's about time you got here."

SUNRISE PEEKED ON the edges of the horizon. The heat of the day would settle in soon and they would have to move. There were plans to make but Connor stood frozen.

He held the jeans Jana laid out to wear. He ran his hands over them and felt around the pockets. The black square in his hand weighed almost nothing but it was heavy against his palm.

The mental battle waged on. Her protection versus his paranoia.

He finally reached a conclusion. It was the right move but the wrong execution. He swore under his breath. "Women."

"What are you doing?"

Her voice had him jumping. Man, no one ever snuck up on him. Just showed how off his game he was around her.

Busted.

He dropped the pants on the mattress. "I'm actually not doing it."

She picked something off the floor and he frowned when he realized it was his old tee. She slipped it over her head and his front-row seat to that amazing body stopped. So did any chance of luring her back between the covers.

Before he could come up with a reasonable explanation, she stood in front of him at the end of the bed. "Are you playing verbal gymnastics in the hope I'll forget I saw you with your hands in my pants?"

Now that was quite a statement. "I like having my hands in your pants."

"No jokes." She folded her arms over her chest. "Talk, and do it now."

The move plumped her breasts and had him getting hard...until she cleared her throat. His gaze flew back to her angry one. "It's a tracker."

"And you were going to sneak it into my clothes." She plucked it out of his hand and held it up, studying it. "Again."

He could see the anger wash over her. Her skin reddened and her mouth fell into a flat line. He knew he only had seconds to make this right. "No."

"Since when do you lie to me?"

That expression, heated and full of fury, had him rushing to explain. "I mean, I was going to then I thought about what you said and how I come on too strong and I stopped."

He tried to do it her way. He'd lost so much by insisting on handling the marriage and her safety on his terms. If she wanted some freedom he'd give it to her. Not now, with gunmen outside. He couldn't control them but he could control his actions. This time he'd planned on talking with her first. Explaining why he needed her to carry the device.

"Really?" Hope threaded through her voice.

He grabbed on to that. "I can be taught, you know."

She glanced around the floor. "Everything but how to hang up your clothes, apparently."

With the simple comment he'd heard so many times before, the tension poured out of him. The battle ended and she believed him. He had to admit that felt pretty damn great. "Picking up clothes is tough for guys."

"Uh-huh." She waved the tracker in front of his face. "So you stopped just short of tracking me without my knowledge."

"Yes. I wanted to tell you first." He couldn't bring himself to say "ask your permission" because if she said no to being tagged he didn't know what he would have done. He was learning but he still understood how to do his job and that tracker was a necessity. "Do I get any credit for that?"

A smile broke over her face. "I think you do."

Crisis averted. The breath rushed out of him in relief. "That wasn't so hard."

"Which is what I've been saying."

Since he guessed he was about to lose ground, he reached for the satphone on the table when it buzzed. He'd grab on to any diversion.

She got to it first and held it up. "I thought we couldn't get calls."

"The bad guys' phones work. I gave Shane and Holt the number and they're passing it around to our side while Joel searches the call logs." Connor clicked the button and put the line on speakerphone. "I'm here with Jana."

Shane skipped the welcomes and went right to the news. "Someone made contact."

Just as Connor thought. Marcel was in this mess up to his eyeballs. "Did he see you?"

"Who?" Jana asked.

Connor ignored the question knowing she would figure it out in a second. Shane must have had the same idea because he answered Connor instead. "I pretended I didn't know he was here."

"Is Marcel still breathing?"

Jana grabbed Connor's arm and tugged. "What did you do?"

He glanced at her, expecting rage and distrust and dreading it. Instead, her eyes narrowed in what looked like confusion. She wasn't yelling or demanding. She wanted to understand. That reality broke through his worries.

But that didn't mean he rushed in. Connor doled out

the information in pieces he thought she could take. She was strong but she believed in Marcel and his cause and wounding her with the truth was not something Connor enjoyed.

"He had a sneak meeting with someone at the house," he explained.

Her expression didn't change but her grip loosened on his arm. "Maybe it's the attackers. He could be hurt. They could have threatened him."

All nice theories but none of them fit the facts. And he sure didn't want her feeling sorry for the guy. "He's in this with them."

She threw up her hands. "How do you know?"

"He didn't call for help and he's still breathing."

Shane mumbled something Connor didn't catch but then Shane's voice rose again. "Unfortunately."

Connor thought the same thing. "Guess we know how the attackers got off the porch so quickly yesterday."

"Yeah," Shane said. "Marcel helped them get away."

That made sense. Connor didn't understand the disappearing act, but now he knew the attackers had a way in and out. Even if Marcel was in danger or being bribed, he let those men in and put them all in danger. That was enough to kill off any sympathy Connor might have had for him.

With her mouth hanging open, she sat down hard on the edge of the bed. "I can't believe this. He runs a charity."

Shane laughed. "So?"

"He *helps* people."

"He's not what you think he is. He's dirty." Connor hoped cutting through the flowery language might help her accept faster. She could mourn later. Be furious tomorrow. Right now he needed her to get on the same page and focus. "And I think it's time I had a serious talk with the man."

Jana bounced right back to her feet. "I'm coming with you."

"No way." Even in this new world where he tried to be understanding and include her in decisions, this one was nonnegotiable.

"Connor."

"I'm going to let him live." He talked over her, not letting her go off on a defense of the man. "For now."

"Then it shouldn't be a problem to have me standing there."

Shane jumped in. "He'll talk more freely if he's not busy trying to defend his actions or trying to win you over, Jana."

She snorted. "That's ridiculous."

Connor appreciated the assist from his friend and ran with it. "Men are simple creatures."

"Speaking of which, let me be there when you punch him." Shane sounded amused by the idea.

Which was a good idea because Connor thought he might need reinforcements to keep from killing Marcel. "Definitely."

She closed her fist around the tracking device. "You have ten minutes then I'm coming in. And there had better not be bloodshed."

No way Connor was agreeing to that.

Chapter Fifteen

Connor walked across the property with Shane by his side, leaving Jana protected by Holt. The sun rose, casting the rocks in a glow of fiery red and orange. The heat of the day would set a few hours from now. This morning a cool breeze settled over the quiet of the abandoned area, causing loose brush to tumble across the landscape.

Their boots thumped in steady precision as both held their guns, fingers off the triggers but close enough to move, if necessary. Rocks and dirt crunched under their matching steps. Neither spoke. They'd trained and run drills without talking, relying on hand signals and matched instincts. They used those skills now.

Keeping his focus on the house, Shane pushed open the front door but hesitated on the threshold. "Remember, you promised Jana not to kill this guy."

"No, I didn't." Out of the corner of his eye, Connor saw Shane smile then it disappeared again.

In front of him, Connor could make out Marcel's outline through the crack in the closed curtains. This guy sent Connor's anger spiking. One look at Marcel's smug face and Connor wanted to hit something. Put the guy in one of those stupid cardigans and let him walk around talking about international politics as if he had any idea what it took behind the scenes to pave a safe way for charities like his and Connor had to fight the urge to give him a reality check.

When they walked in, Marcel stood in the middle of his family room. At the click of their heels, he spun around and jumped. Coffee spilled over his hand. For once, his crafted image slipped and he swore and scowled. Almost seemed human for a second.

Satisfaction surged through Connor. "You're up early."

"What do you want?"

He'd had warmer welcomes, but he'd honestly had worse. At least this one didn't come with a swinging blade or gunfire. "A conversation."

Marcel jumped back as he shook his arm, sending drops of coffee flying, and then wiped his wet hand on his perfectly pressed gray pants. "It's not exactly easy to concentrate. There are a lot of people in the house right now."

The voice, the wardrobe… It all struck Connor as overkill. Normal people got more upset about a kidnapping in their office than spilled coffee. Not this guy. "Not now."

Marcel's scowl deepened. "What?"

For years Connor tried to figure out what Jana saw in Marcel. His accent went in and out. He came off as phony and pretentious, even while walking in squalor in developing countries. Connor tagged the guy as a rich boy who never shook off the entitled attitude of his youth.

Not that the charity didn't do good work. It absolutely did. But Jana could ensure vaccines for those who needed them without depending on this guy to do it.

"Let's not be overly dramatic. Your house isn't swarming with people." Connor nodded in Shane's direction. "There's just the three of us."

Shane made a clicking sound with his tongue as he gave Connor the once-over. "To be fair, you're not exactly small."

"True." And Connor wouldn't hesitate to use that power to protect what mattered most to him.

Marcel put his mug down on the coffee table with a loud clank. "Where's Jana?"

He said it like a demand. The tone had the words skidding across Connor's brain. Heat rose and he itched to put his hand on his gun. "You mean my wife."

"Of course. Who else would I be talking about?" Marcel slid onto the end of the couch. With one leg over the other, he rotated his ankle.

His stance seemed more suited to a party than a talk about keeping his hands and mind off another man's wife. As if Marcel didn't know and couldn't see Connor seething right in front of him.

Connor struggled to keep his voice even. He would not give this weasel the satisfaction of knowing he pricked him. "Just making sure you understood the reality."

The foot stopped bouncing. "What are you talking about?"

"She's taken." Whether Marcel liked it or not, whether Jana understood it or not, she belonged with him. Connor would spend the rest of his life making sure that happened.

Walk away from Corcoran. Put down the weapons. Move, go on vacation, even pick up his clothes. Whatever it took, the part of his life where he lived away from his wife was over. His patience had long expired on that.

"You act like Jana doesn't get a say in what happens in her life," Marcel said. "She's a grown-up."

Shane moved before Connor could. With his legs apart and one hand hovering near his holster like a character in some sort of old-time western, Shane waited as if willing Marcel to push one more time. "He's not getting it."

"Clearly." One word. That was all Connor could get out while holding on to the edge of civility.

"I assume you're trying to tell me something." Marcel drummed his fingers on the armrest of the couch. "Maybe you should come out and say it."

Fine. If he wanted truth, Connor decided to give it to him. Bare and stripped down to the basic point. "Your interest in Jana is over."

The room went still. Marcel's fake smile ripped through the tension a second later. "We only work together. My interest in her is professional."

The guy didn't look like he believed it. Even if he had, Connor would not have bought it. "Right."

Marcel's eyes narrowed as he leaned forward with his elbows on his knees. "That's what this is about, right? You're jealous."

The word grated against Connor's last nerve. Marcel didn't deserve a minute of his time. If Connor was right, the guy had his hands in something nasty and brought Jana along with him.

The job and the personal side mixed and colored everything. Connor had trouble separating out one from the other and staying neutral about any of it.

Most of all, Connor hated Marcel. Everything he said and how he acted. The way Jana made excuses for him. "I'm tired of you hanging around her."

"She came to me." Marcel tapped his fingertips together. "Or is that the real problem? She could go anywhere but she picked me. Over you."

Shane shook his head. "Let me hit him."

Connor considered the possibility but quickly discarded it. Jana would be upset and he lived to make her happy.

"I understand you're upset about the state of your marriage, but don't blame me." Marcel kept tapping. "I didn't do anything to push Jana away. I'm not the one who caused her to run across the country for a break."

That counted as the one step too far. For Jana's sake, Connor held back from unleashing the rage boiling inside him but his control started crumbling. "You might want to tread carefully."

"He carries a gun," Shane pointed out.

Marcel's gaze flicked between the two men towering over him. After a charged silence, he spoke again, this time with a lot less amusement in his voice. "I offered a shoulder and an ear. She had concerns and complaints and I listened."

No way. She left and got angry but Connor refused to believe she used this man—one she knew Connor hated—as a confidant about the most private pieces of marital life. "You expect me to believe that Jana talked to you about me?"

"Well, she has been here for a few months."

"A few months out of a lifetime. Not really important in the grand scheme of things, now is it?" He believed that. He had to or he'd stop functioning.

"Especially since you failed to keep her safe," Shane said.

Marcel's gaze roamed again. "There was a break-in. Not something expected way out here. Frustrating and upsetting but not life ending."

This time Shane and Connor shared a look. Connor wondered if the rage simmering in Shane's eyes would be mirrored in his own.

"Armed men touched her." Connor heard her panicked screams every time he closed his eyes. The sound of her terror would replay in his head until the day he died. Maybe he needed the reminder of how close he came to losing her. Or maybe he deserved the punishment for not guaranteeing her safety, no matter what.

"What do you mean?" Marcel came up off the couch in a rush.

Shane held out a hand, suggesting he was plenty close enough. "You're unclear of the definition of touch?"

"You mean—"

Enough playing around and circling for the right position. Connor went in for the kill. "When she needed someone to help her, she called me. She will always call me."

"If you think you can threaten me—"

"Oh, I definitely can." Can and would.

"Gentlemen. Sorry I'm late."

Connor sensed her before he heard her. Soft footsteps fell on the hardwood floor. He closed his eyes at the sound of her voice and when he opened them again, she stood beside him. With her hair in a ponytail and her face scrubbed clean she looked fresh, younger than she was. The slim blue jeans and light blue polo top helped.

He shifted to include her in their informal circle. "No worries. We were just talking."

Shane shrugged. "Men hanging out. The usual stuff."

"Where's Holt?" Connor asked, even though he could guess the answer.

She smiled. "Keeping watch on the front porch."

Marcel stayed quiet. He stood there staring at Jana. His gaze swept over her and some of the tension left his face.

Connor gauged the distance away from Marcel and thought he could land a punch without much trouble. "Actually, we've been coming to an understanding."

"About?" She stepped closer until her arm touched his.

Connor loved the way she leaned into him. No distance or pretending. "The charity. Marcel agreed to open up all his books and let us pore through everything."

Shane nodded. "He's very helpful."

"I bet." Jana dragged out the words. "Certainly looks like you've come to an understanding."

They all stared at Marcel now. Three sets of eyes focused on him as the blood ran out of his face.

He cleared his voice and returned the glaring then he focused on Jana. "You know I can't do that. There are privacy concerns."

Last thing Connor wanted was Marcel working directly on Jana. She felt bad for the guy and didn't buy into his seediness. If that meant Connor had to keep dragging the conversation back to him, he would. "I'm not going to tell anyone anything."

"That's not the point. I can't just—"

"Yes." She looped her hand through Connor's arm as she backed her former boss down. "You can."

Score one for Jana.

"Excuse me?" Marcel's usual cool demeanor abandoned him as he stuttered out the question.

"I'm not a charity employee, not technically, not anymore, and I've been going through the records. You never complained."

"I thought you were working on outreach. You took on the paperwork issue without telling me."

"Well, reality is I did take it on and have been all over the files and you didn't stop me. If needed I can vouch for my husband." She squeezed Connor's arm. "He has a security clearance and is the most trustworthy man you'll ever meet."

Connor was pretty sure she'd never been hotter. "Thank you, honey."

"I'm sorry, but your word is not good enough. There are liability issues at work here. You know that."

"Then there's the part where Connor has a gun," Shane said.

"They need the information to provide the proper level of protection. This is not about getting access to credit card numbers or scamming anyone." She dropped her hand. "More importantly, the task will go faster with Connor's help. We can all agree that everyone suffers if the charity isn't up and operational. The sooner we get through this, the better."

Connor had the exact same thought. "In other words, she wants to be done so she can come home. With me."

"That is not what she said."

The words didn't matter. Not to Connor. "It's what's happening."

"That's her decision." Marcel practically screamed his comment.

Connor let it float there. If Marcel wanted to prove he viewed himself as a friend only, he'd come pretty close to blowing it. Even Jana frowned at him now. She didn't ruffle. She stood there, soaking it all in and looking as if she was fighting off a men-are-so-ridiculous eyeroll.

"If it's my decision, we're going. Get whatever you need and we'll head over to the charity." When Marcel started to talk over her, she cut him off. "Please, Marcel."

Connor almost felt bad for the guy. Ignoring her when she asked like that proved impossible for Connor. Her eyes grew big and soft and he got dragged under. Looked like Marcel suffered from the same reaction.

His shoulders fell. "I'll meet you there."

Shane dropped down on the arm of Marcel's couch. "I'll wait here and drive you."

"That's not necessary," Marcel said through clenched teeth.

So much for Marcel's carefully crafted calm. The guy folded and his anger raged. This act differed from the one he usually tried to sell. Connor thought it was about time. "There are killers on the loose."

Shane smiled. "We'd hate to see anything happen to you."

"Jana, may I speak to you for a second?" Marcel took a step toward Jana.

She backed up before he could touch her. "We'll talk at the office."

LUC DIDN'T BOTHER with niceties and introductions. He'd been waiting in his secure space under the house and heard the entire pathetic conversation. Connor roped Marcel in and ran him around in circles until he cracked. Then Jana stepped in and smacked the final nail in the coffin.

It was embarrassing, really. The whole scene made Luc wonder how Marcel had run this operation for as long as he had. It also convinced him that today was it. They had to run the final plan and get out.

With the decision made, Luc contacted the men. Now he had to explain to Marcel. Luc went back and forth and decided limited information was the answer. Let Marcel think he was in charge. He had set up the entire vaccines-as-cover scheme to begin with, but he'd long ago been shifted out of top management and used for his contacts only. Not that he understood the change in the balance of power.

The second Connor and the gang left, Luc stepped into the hallway. He had only a few minutes since Shane made it clear he'd be coming back and even now was talking with Connor on the front porch. Probably planning some military incursion, knowing those two.

Marcel dropped his mug in the kitchen sink. With the force of the thud, Luc half expected it to shatter. Instead, it thudded and spun as Marcel balanced his hands on the edge of the counter. He didn't turn around and Luc didn't signal his arrival.

Marcel's shoulders stiffened as a slicing sound whizzed through the air. When he spun around he had a knife in his hand. He blew out a hard breath as he set the blade on the counter with a shaking hand.

Marcel's harsh intake of breath cut off. "What's wrong with you?"

"Keep your voice down." Having Shane and Connor come in with guns blazing would not go well for any of them. Luc could open fire but he predicted Marcel would be a hindrance in any stress-filled situation.

"You can't just come in and out of my house."

"You knew I was here." He had been in and out of the house. Part of him liked the thrill and the danger. Proving over and over that he could walk in right under the Corcoran Team's noses was a side benefit.

"I thought you snuck out." Marcel leaned against the counter. "Where's Bruce?"

Luc was getting pretty sick of everyone acting like Bruce had the tactical lead on this operation. The guy came on board for this one job. Being handpicked by the boss had its perks but Luc was ready for him to leave. "Handling some of the details for later."

As usual, Marcel didn't ask what those were. He wanted things done and didn't care how they were done so long as he didn't have to hear about them. That lack of commitment only made Luc outline every detail to torture Marcel. He'd been about to do just that before they heard the heavy footsteps on the porch and Connor walked in.

Pushing this guy off his high pedestal was the only decent part of this job so far. So Luc intended to keep doing it.

"This time you need to be successful."

"About that." There was no way Luc would take the fall for any failure in this operation. Not when the blame fell so easily on other shoulders. "Seems like you forgot to mention an important fact."

Marcel waved him off. "I can handle Connor Bowen."

"Really?" Luc had had a front-row seat and watched a professional toying with a novice. At another time, in another situation, preferably one that couldn't trace back to him and land him in prison, Luc may have enjoyed watching Marcel get wrapped up in his obsession and lies. Not this time.

Marcel might view himself as some sort of international power player but no one else did. Until recently he'd been married and in a constant state of panic over being caught using his charity as a cover. He whined and lost focus. He provided the basis, the shipments perfect for the crates and merchandise they really needed to move. But that was the only pro in his column.

"I'm playing a role as a director of a charity," Marcel said. "Being what Connor expects."

Not that Luc saw. To the extent Marcel ever had a convincing cover it appeared to be blown now. And that made him a liability.

Luc decided to lay it out. "You're in love with his wife and he knows it."

"That's not true."

"It's clear what you want to do to her and it's nasty."

"You're out of line." Marcel's voice rose and shook as he talked.

"Keep it down." Luc struggled to maintain a whisper over his growing frustration.

"Then stop talking about Jana."

As far as Luc was concerned, the lack of communication about her was the problem. "Don't you think I needed to know what was happening between you two before we started this operation?"

That was the one thing Luc could not tolerate. He'd put his reputation, not to mention his life, on the line. All for some lovesick idiot who couldn't keep his focus long enough to finish a job.

Marcel pushed off from the counter. "You had the facts you needed. You're the one who's failed to accomplish even the most simple of tasks in this operation."

"Because I wasn't permitted to cut through this and hurt Jana. Now I know why." The calculation struck Luc as obvious. He just needed to talk fast enough when the time came to keep the spotlight on Marcel and prevent it from shifting.

A creak had them both turning toward the front of the house. Luc reached for his gun and Marcel grabbed a pot. So long as the noise didn't lead to footsteps they'd be fine. For a few more seconds they stayed quiet and unmoving. Nothing happened. Whatever drew their attention sounded like it hadn't breached the door.

Marcel stepped forward and looked down the hall to the front door. "Probably the porch."

"Fix that before it causes trouble."

"Right, I'll get to it in my spare time since I have so much of that." Marcel looked out the window to the side of the kitchen area.

"You're welcome to join us on the front lines outside. Just make sure you duck when the bullets start flying." Luc did not want to hear about how hard the work was from the guy who sat at a desk all day.

"You shouldn't be in here."

Luc wasn't ready to let this go. This was too important and impacted too many people. Some who knew who to shoot and tended to get blinded by anger. "Does everyone know about your crush on Jana but me?"

"That's enough." Marcel's voice dropped back to a soft whisper. "We're done talking about this."

This guy still didn't get it. This wasn't a game. "I've lost a lot of men out here."

"Which says something about the people you hire."

They'd suffered real losses that would set back their operation. That sort of thing destroyed morale. It also made busywork that Luc didn't need. Searching through lists of mercenaries to find qualified people amounted to a waste of time. He'd do it because he had to, but he'd much rather blame someone else.

"What about your choices? You bring your girlfriend here and she uncovers everything." The level of stupidity involved in that socked Luc. He decided right there he needed new partners on the next job.

This time Marcel didn't deny his dream relationship with Jana. "Not everything. She thinks there's a math error in the paperwork. No big deal."

If that were true they wouldn't have a stack of bodies outside and undercover operatives swarming the place. Luc didn't know why Marcel couldn't see that. "I disagree."

"I can convince her."

The man continued to wallow in cluelessness. "She's not stupid."

"I'll direct her where I need her to go." Marcel gave another sneak peek at the front of the house. "I've done it before."

As far as Luc could see, Marcel ignored one very important factor in all of this. What he'd come to see as *the* biggest factor. "Even if that's true, you can't control her husband."

"His time is almost over."

Sounded as if Marcel planned to beak protocol and remove Connor. Luc wanted to be there to see that because he couldn't imagine it. "That's what this has all been about. All the planning and the hiring of muscle to help out. You came up with this elaborate scheme to lure him here, get rid of the competition and become the hero."

"All of this has been about tying up loose ends. Connor is the ultimate loose end. Trust me."

"No." Killing Connor would bring down the wrath of his men. Luc didn't want that much attention and he knew he would not be alone on that.

"You have one final chance to do your job."

Threats. Those qualified as Luc's least favorite things. "Or?"

"You think the paperwork won't lead back to you? That I don't have this all figured out?" Marcel's hubris snapped back into place. He delivered his speech in a voice filled with satisfaction. "I've been doing this a long time."

"I thought you were retiring." That was part of the plan. Marcel planned to walk away with his reputation intact and a lot of money in his pocket.

So did Luc. That was the piece that kept him from unloading. Marcel thought he had his ticket out, but Luc had a contingency in place. One where he would not be implicated. Others would pay and he would walk away. With the money.

The man made one threat too many. Threw around big words and acted like he could dictate what happened from here on out. As if Luc could let him live now.

"I am getting out and will not be looking over my shoulder for Connor Bowen. The only way to ensure that doesn't happen is to eliminate him."

It was the way Marcel said it. So sure with an almost stupid dreamy expression. He'd clearly spun some strange romantic fantasy that included a woman who worked for him and appeared to think of him as nothing more than a mentor.

Luc had to hold back a laugh at the other man's expense. "But you plan to take his wife with you. You actually think she'll walk away from her husband and her life and be with you?"

"She already did."

The signs were so obvious yet he kept missing them. "You're not paying attention because that woman is not on the verge of leaving her husband. Not even close."

"She's not your concern."

Luc didn't understand it. It was as if this one woman choked off all common sense and cost them more bodies on this mission. "Fine, but you need to know this is about to go down."

"Good."

Luc talked right over Marcel. "The plan is now in play and can't be pulled back."

"So?"

"If it comes down to killing her or getting out of this without trouble, I will put a bullet right in the middle of that pretty forehead."

Marcel straightened. "No one touches her."

Luc was done agreeing to nonsense. "You heard what I said."

Chapter Sixteen

Jana's head pounded hard enough to block her hearing. She'd wanted to yell at Connor during the short drive to the charity office. He'd waltzed into Marcel's house and did the macho-guy thing. Flexed muscles and threw around phrases like *my woman,* or maybe he hadn't, but it sure sounded like it from where she listened in on the porch.

But one thing had changed. She could no longer pretend Marcel looked on her as if they were in some sort of mentor relationship. He hadn't come right out and admitted his feelings for her, but she picked up on the clues. His voice changed and he grew stern. An emotion she couldn't name had washed over him, stripping away the charming facade she knew.

The way he looked at her when she walked into the room. The suggestion she had shared her feelings about her marriage, which she absolutely had not. The things he'd said about Connor making a huge mistake in letting her go. Marcel had started dropping those comments a few weeks ago.

It all made sense now. Marcel wanted something more. Something she would never give him.

After pulling up to the charity and putting the car in Park, Connor got out and slammed the driver's-side door. Instead of going into the building he folded an arm on the top of the car and stared at her over the roof. "Are you not talking to me?"

"Why would I be mad?" She didn't know what she was other than confused and frustrated.

"Well, there's the thing where you just used the word mad."

She'd put her marriage on hold and went searching. A man she trusted to give her shelter had ulterior motives. It looked like her husband's jealousy had some foundation. Every way she could mess up and get things wrong, she had. The enormity of it made her dizzy. She reached out for the car to regain her balance.

"You promised not to attack Marcel." She heard the slap of the accusation in her voice. She hadn't meant to say anything.

"He's still alive, isn't he?"

She couldn't handle this. Not now. Thoughts and regret spun in her head. She doubted every decision she'd made over the past few months and questioned her judgment. If Marcel really was using the charity to do something illegal, she might just strangle him and let Connor watch.

She had to know and the only way to do that was to step back into that building. The same one where men had chased her and dragged her off.

Pulling up a well of strength she wasn't sure she had, she stood up straight and headed for the front door. "Let's just do this."

Connor met her on the bottom stair and matched his step to hers. "I would point out I didn't make up his feelings for you. This was not just about me losing my temper or being unreasonable, though I admit I have been that at times. You want me to say you made me jealous? Fine, you did."

She hated that. She was not that kind of woman. She didn't get any joy out of making Connor miserable. That for a second he believed she cheated or would play games to have it look that way made her sick for him.

It also made her a little angry. She would never do that and at least *that* he should know. "I told you I don't view him that way."

The wind carried her hair and Connor reached out and tucked it behind her ear. The touch was so gentle and loving that tears pushed against the backs of her eyes.

"But he thinks of you as his girlfriend." Connor said the words in a soft voice, as if it hurt to mutter them.

She caught his hand and held it. "I'm not."

"I'm not the one you need to convince."

She sensed that was true. After all of her denials to Connor, she now had to sit Marcel down and tell him the score. She'd assumed he knew the truth, but now she was sure that wasn't true.

She kissed his hand then dropped it. "Let's just focus on the charity issues right now. One problem at a time."

"Am I the problem or is Marcel?"

It looked like Connor wasn't ready to move on and handle something else. Her chest ached at the thought. "You're both being difficult right now."

He came to a stop and his shoes scraped against the rough ground. "Tell me again. What exactly did I do in the last half hour that's the problem?"

She took in the frown and the square shoulders. He looked ready for battle and ten seconds from launching into a new litany of anti-Marcel information. She didn't want to listen. Disappointment already weighed down her muscles and exhausted her.

Still, Connor deserved to know one truth. "You were right about him."

"What?"

"You heard me. I'm not repeating it."

Connor's head shot forward and his eyes went to tiny slits. Then it all changed. A smile pushed up one side of his mouth and those sexy eyes went wide. "Ahh."

Yeah, now he got it. She admitted it. He was right and she was wrong. And… "I hate that."

That smile went to full wattage. "I'd apologize—"

"We can add this to all the mistakes I've made lately. The pile is getting pretty huge." She couldn't even think about the long list without wanting to sit down.

His mouth fell flat again. He reached for her as she went up the two steps to the door. "Jana, that's not—"

With her hand on the knob, she turned around and faced him again. Her back touched the door but she didn't bolt. Even though she really wanted to. "You have every right to rub it in."

A few thuds of his footsteps and he stood in front of her. "I'd rather kiss you."

The pressure behind her gave and the door opened. She would have flown backward but a firm hand caught her shoulder and Connor grabbed her arms. For a second, fear flashed through her. The memories of the kidnapping flooded back. Then a strong arm wrapped around her.

Cam squeezed her close to his side. "I get a hug first."

"For what?" She looked him over, admiring every impressive inch. Brown hair and that cute dimple in his cheek. The ladies took one look at the former black ops expert and started fixing their hair and applying lipstick. Not that he noticed.

He smiled down at her. "Surviving the jeep explosion and run through the desert."

"Sounds like a normal day for you guys, but I'm happy you're all okay." And she was because she loved every last alpha, demanding one of them.

Cam looked from her to Connor and back again. "Does that mean you're coming home?"

"Feel free to answer the man so long as the answer is yes," Connor said.

If they could get through this and find time to sit down and talk through all the things they'd skimmed over in the past, she was. She hated being away from the house and Connor. She wanted her life back. She needed him to understand she was a wife and not a client who needed protecting.

For months she thought she needed time away. She'd been wrong and she had to own that. What she really needed was Connor. Turned out loving him was easy. Living with him was not but they could make rules and loosen the string. At least she hoped that was true.

"I am not having a conversation about my personal life until whatever is happening here is resolved." She relaxed all of her other dealing-with-the-husband rules over the past few days. She was determined to hold firm on this one.

Cam made a face. Even threw in a hissing sound as his arm dropped away from her. "About that."

"What?" Connor asked.

"Let's head in." Cam opened the door and ushered them inside. "Drake and I found some paperwork in the safe."

The inside looked like a windstorm passed through. There were papers everywhere and boxes and smashed bits of…she wasn't even sure what. A wall, maybe? Anxiety whirred to life inside her. The men. The chase. The call to Connor. She wanted to forget it all.

"How did you get it open?" Not that she got an answer. She got staring and a bit of an are-you-kidding-me look. "Right, forget I asked."

Cam walked over to a table with neat stacks of files and

papers on it. He grabbed a few off the top. "Looks like Marcel is using the shipments to carry something other than vaccines overseas—"

"No." It was a reflex response. She said it but while she studied the paper in Connor's hand she realized she'd never seen it before. It looked different from the other invoices and included Marcel's handwriting and specifically referenced the unaccounted-for additional boxes.

Connor handed the document to her. His stern expression and the way his skin pulled tight across his mouth showed his inner turmoil. "I know this is difficult to take in, but he's dirty."

She understood this looked bad and she guessed Marcel was doing something secretive and likely pretty awful. She couldn't really deal with that idea so she locked it away in another part of her brain. Later she'd take all the information out and assess it. If this was like the last time when the charity was being used or if anything else was happening under her nose, she'd wrestle with that guilt and her failings later.

Now she needed focus to get at the thought that kept nibbling at her. "You told me your friend has been watching over the shipments. How would Marcel be moving extra boxes of anything from here, directing and hiding, with the oversight you set up?"

"What are you talking about?" Cam asked.

Connor stared at her for an extra second before breaking off to glance at Cam. "You know this charity has had issues before, right?"

"Sure. That was your last job before starting Corcoran. The one where you met Jana."

"After that, since Jana still did work for the charity even from afar, I called in some favors and Drake agreed to act like a watchdog. The distribution chains tend to be in the rough areas where he works."

"For the CIA." She filled in the blank in case Cam didn't know. But when he didn't so much as blink, she guessed Cam might have more inside information on Connor's past than she did.

"Sort of." Connor waved a hand in front of his face. "That doesn't matter now."

"Wait a second." Cam shifted his weight. "Why didn't Drake tell me that when we were going through all of the documents and coming up with potential scenarios?"

That was exactly Jana's question. This guy had all these skills but missed potential drug running or illegal distribution of some type happening right in front of him? That didn't make any sense to her.

"He probably thought he was keeping my confidence." Connor's expression didn't change but something in his voice did. "Where is he?"

"Holt got here before you and they went out checking for tracks and evidence."

Connor nodded at the satphone. "Call them in."

LUC PUSHED DOWN the excitement welling inside him as he lined up the gunsight. They'd rotated through so many plans that he'd lost count by this point. He wasn't even sure what the end goal was. On one hand they wanted Jana to stop snooping and Connor stopped before he picked up the trail she'd found. On the other, they wanted Connor. For what, Luc didn't really know.

Regardless of the final solution, they'd all failed. But this one would work. Separate and destroy. It was so simple. Don't let the Corcoran Team members gather or get too close. Pick them off one by one.

And this was the first domino. From here they'd give

the okay for the next attack. When the smoke cleared only Connor would be standing and only long enough to see his wife go down.

It was a shame, really. A beautiful woman like that deserved a chance to change sides, but the boss wanted her gone now. Too much had happened. Too much time had been lost and too many men had been killed.

He stood at the bedroom window and looked through his sight again. He had a clear shot of this guy Shane's back as he walked the grounds of Marcel's property with his head down. At this distance with this rifle it would only take one shot.

Shane stopped, facing away. The man almost made it too easy.

"I'll take him." One shot. No wasted ammunition and certainly no opportunity for Shane to return fire.

Marcel hovered too close. For a guy who wanted clean hands he was almost cheering for this putdown. "Quick and clean. We need to get over to the charity office."

Luc knew the plan. Hell, he'd created the plan. He didn't need either a cheerleader or someone pretending to be in charge when he wasn't. "No problem."

"He took his vest off." Marcel shook his head. "Stupid."

The desert heat started burning and Shane had stripped it off. Luc stood right there and watched. Now the vest rested on a chair only a few feet away from him. Not that it would help him there. "I guess these Corcoran guys aren't as smart as everyone says."

Luc got into shooting position. He ran through the checklist in his mind.

Marcel's hand darted over and he lowered the weapon. "What are you doing?"

"Like I just said, taking a shot." It took every ounce of

control Luc possessed not to shoot Marcel. "And never touch my gun."

"From here?"

From the way Marcel looked around his bedroom, Luc guessed the other man didn't like the choice of shooting position right near his pillow. That was tough because this room gave Luc the best angle. "You wanted quick."

Before Marcel could whine or do something to draw attention to them, Luc aimed and fired. There was a crack and the man dropped. The broad shoulders tipped forward and the rest of his body followed. A whoosh and he went boneless.

Satisfaction surged through Luc. He'd missed that sensation on this job. So many steps had gone wrong. But not this one. This time he could enjoy the win.

He looked at the still form crumpled on the red land for a few seconds. "Done."

"That's not what I expected."

"Get used to it since he's just the first." Luc ignored Marcel and lowered the weapon. "Now it's time for Phase Two."

Chapter Seventeen

Holt called in and said he was on the way in with Drake. They'd tracked the men who held Jana through the canyon then lost the trail. Not a surprise. The weather and the attackers' training made finding any evidence in that direction a longshot. But since they were turning over everything and Drake's tracking skills qualified as the best Connor had even known, Connor gave it a try.

With everyone checking in, he stood by the charity's front door and did a visual sweep of the area. A few cars littered the driveway, including an extra one Jana said Marcel kept at the office for the workers' use. The heat swirled around them, more intense than usual for this time of year, and blurred the air.

The vast openness stretched out in front of them. After a few seconds, Holt and Drake appeared in the distance. They walked across a boulder and through a patch of pure sand. Their strides matched and both had that lethal "don't mess with me" look.

Jana shaded her eyes with her hand as she watched. "That's Drake?"

"Yes." Seeing his former colleague usually worked to ease some of Connor's anxiety. Not this time.

He didn't understand the lapse of surveillance or possible missteps that let Marcel get away with whatever he was doing. Having the charity cheat and steal was bad enough but this time Jana got sucked in.

After all those years working outside the country and sleeping in a series of rotating safe houses, it was possible the nomadic, no-commitments life had taken its toll. Connor couldn't believe Drake stayed in this long. Could be it was time for him to get out.

"You haven't met him?" Cam called out the question from behind them inside the office.

She shook her head as the men moved closer. "Never."

They drew within fifteen feet when Drake turned around. Connor followed his gaze to the sedan driving down the dirt road. They went hours in this area without seeing a car. Now someone headed their way right as they were meeting up. He didn't like coincidences and this struck him as a serious one.

"It's Marcel," Jana said, for once not sounding too excited about his arrival.

The time in Utah basically sucked. But if getting Jana out and home and clear of Marcel happened, it would all be worth it. Connor just wanted the job done. He wouldn't be able to relax until he put the pieces together and figured out who wanted him and Jana, and why.

"I did tell him to get here." Connor tried to make out who was inside and cursed his decision to leave the binoculars back in the room. "Cam, call Shane and see if he's with Marcel."

"Will do."

They all watched the approaching car. When a roaring sound echoed off to Connor's left it took him a second to realize it was an engine. It revved and thundered, but this didn't come from the approaching car. Wrong direction and wrong noise.

No, this came from the vehicle parked in front of them. The one without a driver.

Before Connor could blink it came barreling right toward them. Jana screamed but her body seemed frozen. He heard banging and smelled something hot and metallic. None of the sights and sounds made sense.

Instinct took over. The car careened and he lunged for Jana. He pulled her toward him and momentum took them flying off to the side. They dove and took flight before slamming into the ground.

Rolling, he heard a ground-shaking crash. With her body tucked under his, they both looked up. Drake and Holt fired on the racing vehicle but it was too late. It crashed into the front of the office.

The roof caved and rafters fell. The bangs rang out over the gunfire. It took a few seconds before the crunch of the wheels against the gravel and debris finally stopped. The building creaked and moaned then a boom knocked Connor down.

The sound, the force of the air and wall of heat rocked him. He tucked Jana's head under his and ignored her squirming. Chunks of the building and parts of the car rained down on them. When one piece got close enough to burn his pants, he rolled them farther out of the way.

The shower of debris finally stopped. The heat and thick air remained. He looked up again to see flames shooting into the sky as they devoured the office's roof. A bomb, an explosion… None of it made sense.

The boom knocked out his hearing. The world came to him muffled now. He heard Holt shouting but couldn't make out the words. He was forgetting something.

"Cam!" Jana screamed the name as she clawed to get out from under Connor.

Until that moment Connor thought they'd all gotten out.

Now he conducted a quick mental roll call and scanned the area. They were one down. Smoke started to billow and Holt ran toward the consuming fire.

Somehow in the fall of rafters and spray of sparks, Marcel's car registered. It pulled close and stopped. Connor expected to see Shane in the driver's seat but it wasn't him. There was no urgency or frantic run into the building. Just two men, neither of them Corcoran men.

"That's the leader." Jana tugged on Connor's arm as she said the words. She scooted back, dragging her butt in the dirt and trying to take Connor with her.

This was the guy who wanted him but Connor still had no idea who he was. That only heightened the danger. He caught her right as a shot pinged into the ground by his foot.

"Move!" Drake yelled from off to Connor's right.

Through the haze and the smoke, Connor got her up. The fuzz cleared from his mind as he dragged her around to the side of the burning building. The two newcomers came onto the scene firing while ducking behind the car. Neither was Marcel.

The open area had turned into a shooting gallery. He and Jana could only run so far before dodging flames. The rapidly spreading fire pinned Holt down by the front door. There was nowhere for him to hide and the fire licked the beams behind him.

Connor tried to focus as he took in every danger. They all needed his help. Cam was down, he had no idea where Shane had disappeared to and Holt was ten seconds away from catching on fire.

Save his men. Cover his woman. The mantra rang in Connor's head as the adrenaline built.

Drake ran over, sliding in beside them and kicking up pebbles as he did. He motioned for Connor to make a dash to grab Holt or at least get close enough to draw the gunfire. Drake would provide cover. They'd done this a hundred times—scatter the attackers' resources and have them trying to handle too many directions at once. As far as diversions went, it was effective. Most times it worked. Connor hoped this would be one.

"Cover her, too." Connor couldn't tell if he yelled the command or whispered it, but Drake nodded.

With a last look at Jana and at the smudges of dirt and sand on her face, he raced toward Holt. He cut in close and the gunfire closed in on him. The break let Holt pull out of the circle of flames dancing around his back. Closer to Connor now, Holt returned fire, never stopping long enough to provide an easy target.

But they were not in the clear. Fire roared behind them and the blinding heat felt as if it was eating away at Connor's clothes. They pivoted until they stood back to back. They kept moving and firing. Spinning and shifting, careful to lead the attackers away from Jana's hiding place.

Connor decided he'd rather take his chances with the bullets than the flames. He at least stood a chance of dodging those. On a silent count of three he moved Holt toward the car, closer to the guns aimed in their direction. At the last second, Holt bolted and landed with his back against the front of the car.

That left the easy shot and Connor took it. Dropping to his stomach he ignored the sound of crashing windows and the thumping of bullets against steel. He shifted until he got the clear sight then shot the attacker right in the leg.

There was a yell and the man went down. Connor nailed him again, this time in the side. The guy's weapon stayed just out of reach but if he lunged for it, he'd grab it. Connor couldn't have that. He heard the scuffle of footsteps as Holt moved but Connor concentrated on the panicked eyes he could see at the other end of the car.

Up and on his feet. Connor reached the attacker's gun as the man's fingers skimmed it. Stepping on his wrist, he pushed down until he heard a crunch and the guy wailed in pain. Sensing he was not alone, Connor glanced up, bringing his gun with him, and looked into the face of the man who supposedly wanted him dead.

"I don't care what the boss wants. You're dead."

The guy took too much time talking. Just enough for Holt to come up behind him and crack him in the head. The guy stumbled but his finger moved to the trigger. Losing consciousness and going down, he still looked ready to fire.

Connor put a bullet in his forehead and made sure that didn't happen.

"Tie up the wounded one," Connor said. "I don't want him crawling out of here."

Holt was already on his knees, getting the job done. "Right."

Cam. No sooner did he think it than Holt turned around and looked at the burning building. They had to go in. At least try to drag their man out. First, Connor's gaze went to Jana. He wanted to do a visual check and make sure she hadn't been injured in their jump away from the car. She wasn't there.

He stared at the spot in the dirt where they fell. He could see the imprints from their bodies and footprints leading away. "What the hell?"

"We need to get..." Holt's gaze followed Connor's. "What?"

"Where did she go?"

"She's still with Drake." The hoarse voice came from the opposite side of the building. Cam made the comment then doubled over in a coughing fit. His clothes were singed and small pieces of burning debris littered his hair.

"Cam?" Holt rushed over and helped out with a few slaps to the back that might have made a weaker man drop to the ground.

Connor was so relieved, so grateful to have Cam standing in front of him. The breath hiccupped right out of him. "How did you get out?"

Cam stood up and inhaled a deep gulp of air. The move set the coughing off again. When he finally wound down he shook his head. "Good thing I was headed for the back door to give us some support from the rear when the car came barreling in."

"It's a really good thing you run fast." Holt gave his friend another cuff on the shoulder.

Relief gave way to dread. Fear and anxiety balled inside Connor. Something wasn't right. The pieces didn't make sense to him and those drag marks had his brain misfiring. Add in the delays and the not moving and he was on edge.

"Where exactly is Jana right now?" Maybe that would explain her reluctance to go there.

Cam eyed his boss. "I thought Drake took her out of the danger zone on your orders."

"No." Maybe he'd said something like that but Connor knew this was something else. That neck ache came back in full force.

The Drake he knew, or thought he knew, wouldn't walk away without warning, even if he meant to protect her. And the drag marks from the one set of tracks suggested Jana didn't go willingly.

Connor tried to concentrate and force the pieces together in his head. The inventory mistakes at the charity. The case all those years ago with similar issues. Then it was about vaccines being sold on the open market as part of the money-making scheme. Now…what?

He didn't know what was in those extra crates but he knew who should be watching over the distribution. And who had a hand in the charity then and now. Marcel and Jana, but there was one other.

Connor added it up and the answer nearly doubled him over.

Holt frowned. "Connor, what's going on?"

"I'm not sure." But he knew. He sensed it. The man he brought in to help, the man he always trusted, was at the bottom of this somehow.

Another car approached. This one a truck Connor recognized and from the yelling over the satphone, he knew they had a new problem. Tires squealed and the truck came in too hot. The erratic driving meant one thing—Shane.

He jumped down and out of the vehicle before he put it in Park. "I have a gift for you, but I warn you, it's pretty crappy."

Shane went around to the passenger side and dragged Marcel out of the seat and across the dirt to stand in front of them. The man's knees buckled but Shane held him up.

Marcel had bruises on his face and blood at the corner of his mouth. With the ripped shirt he didn't look like his usual poseur self.

Connor had to fight from tearing the man apart. "What's this?"

"He and his friend shot me in the back." Shane said it so matter-of-factly, as if he'd been expecting it and disappointed to be right.

Holt's eyebrow rose. "The vest trick worked?"

Connor knew his mind wandered and he wanted to get moving, but he'd lost the conversation and this could matter, so he tried to tune back in. "What?"

"I knew this was coming. This one wanted me dead and out of the way for whatever they were hatching over here. I see it had some firepower to it." Shane shoved Marcel and the man went down hard on his knees in the dirt. "I had an extra vest and made a show of walking around the yard without the one they expected me to wear. Kept my head down and waited for the cowards to shoot me in the back, and they did."

"At least you had the extra vest." Holt scowled at Marcel. "They tried to set me on fire."

Cam brushed the ashes out of his hair. "I almost got wiped out by a car."

They could celebrate their victories later. Right now, Connor wanted answers and some intel before he went racing after his wife.

He turned on Marcel, lifting the guy's head up and forcing him to look at his captors. "You ready to talk now?"

"It was all Drake." The words bubbled out of Marcel now. Gone was the sneer and condescension. He'd been broken and if the state of him was any indication, Shane actually made a run at literally making that happen. "The weapons. We used the shipments to smuggle weapons. Sold them on the black market."

Holt stepped in real close. "We should kill you."

"Not yet." Not ever, but Marcel didn't need to know that. He could wet himself with fear for all Connor cared. "You were both in on it last time—you and Drake—weren't you? Jana figured it out then, too, only you were really bad at covering your tracks back then. This time you kept the shipments small to make them harder to track."

"They were supposed to be random, but our buyers had needs."

"And you did them at specific intervals. Jana saw the pattern. She just didn't believe you could be so disgusting."

Connor hadn't made that mistake. He'd screwed up when it came to Drake but not Marcel. Connor had always seen through Marcel.

He just missed the more obvious villain at his back. All those years… Connor shook his head, trying to force out the memories. He couldn't get swamped with emotions now. He needed a clear head to get his wife back.

They weren't going up against a novice. Drake had skills that rivaled theirs. He likely also thought he'd killed some of them, so they had the advantage of numbers.

Marcel swallowed. "This was my last job. I was cleaning things up when Jana arrived."

"You should have sent her away," Cam said, his voice deadly calm.

"He couldn't." Shane grabbed a fist full of Marcel's shirt. "He wanted her for himself."

Connor needed one more piece before they could move. "Keep talking. Why does Drake want her?"

"He knew she'd eventually tell you and you'd put it all together. You'd add up what happened in the past and put it together that he ran the whole thing."

"Why not take Jana out?" Cam asked.

Marcel never broke eye contact with Connor. "Because you would never stop."

"That's right." He leaned down and met the man face-to-face. "There's one more thing you should know."

Marcel squirmed and tried to back up but Shane had a death grip on him. "Hold still. If she's hurt, if she even has a hangnail, I'm going to gut you." Connor meant every word.

The last of Marcel's composure slipped. He half cried and half begged. "I… You can't…"

Holt rolled his eyes. "Shut up."

"How do we find her?" Cam asked.

That was the easy part. Now that his head had cleared and he had focus, Connor didn't need help with this. "I know exactly where she is."

Shane shot Connor a narrowed-eye look of disbelief but then it cleared and one of his eyebrows lifted. "You put another tracker on her?"

"No, I showed it to her and she put it in her pocket." Connor had never been so grateful for anything in his life. He let her have the choice and she made it and now it would save her.

He'd deal with the guilt of his friendship with Drake putting her in danger later. Now he'd focus on the rescue.

Holt laughed. "Always did love that woman."

"You are not alone in that." Connor pointed at Marcel. "Put him in the truck. He's coming with us."

Chapter Eighteen

Jana looked around for anything she could use as a weapon. Drake had dragged her from the office to a car waiting nearby. The ride in the trunk had been short, which gave her plenty of time to mentally berate her reaction. Drake had whispered something to her back at the fire about being safe and she froze.

That voice had played in her mind ever since the kidnapping, just waiting for her to have something to compare it to. Then she heard it. Soft but still so clear. She never expected one of Connor's oldest friends would be the attacker. Would want her dead and Connor pleading for her life.

Drake loaded a bag onto the helicopter but his other hand stayed on the gun. "I knew you recognized my voice."

"You were the one behind me when I was tied to the chair." There was no reason to pretend now. He'd showed his hand and she had nothing left to lose…except her life.

But Connor wouldn't let that happen. He'd remember the scene in the bedroom and the tracker and find her. He just had to notice her gone and battle whatever grief and guilt might attack him first.

"I couldn't afford to let you hear me. Well, until now. Now it doesn't matter." Drake dumped a second bag next to the first.

She didn't know where they were or when he brought a helicopter in. She didn't see a pilot but if he was like the Corcoran team members, he could fly certain planes. These men had skills across the board.

Realizing Drake possessed them too set off a new burst of panic inside her. She had to push that all back and force her teeth not to chatter from the fear.

Connor taught her not to let the terror show. Relax, stay calm and collect intel. Stall and no matter what, do not let someone get you in a car. She'd already violated that but she assumed the rule applied to helicopters as well and planned to win that round.

She glanced around at the desolate area. Brush tumbled past in the slight wind and towering rocks lined the distance. They stood in a lower-lying area, almost flat and filled mostly with smaller stones and rough trails where the elements had worn paths into the ground.

"Why?"

He didn't pretend to be confused. "Because this operation is over."

"You were running drugs in those extra crates." Her voice shook as she said the words. That came from anger, not fear. Kids needed the immunizations and he turned a simple act of charity into a money-making scheme.

"Guns."

The word didn't make any sense to her. "What?"

"There's more money in weapons these days."

The reality of the scheme hit her full on in the chest. "It was you at the beginning."

"Beginning, middle and the end. Thanks to you, the formal end to this operation, one that has gone on and funded me for years, is here." He frowned at her. "As you might imagine, I am not happy about that."

One thought ran through her head. Bad guys should

look like bad guys. People should be able to point them out and stay clear. This guy was every inch the good soldier. He had the all-American good looks. There was nothing disgusting and scary about him in an overt way like there had been with that one kidnapper.

No, Drake seemed normal, likeable. Objectively attractive. And that false persona made him all the more dangerous.

"You kidnapped me to hurt Connor?" And not protecting her would destroy him. He ran drills and drove them apart over the issue. To find out he'd let his guard down would break him. Never mind that she walked away and stepped out of his safe cocoon.

"I had my people grab you because, once again, you were nosing around where you shouldn't have been. You know, I thought when Connor married you and you dragged him away from his career—"

Rage heated her skin from the inside out. "I didn't."

"I was there, Jana."

"So was I. Connor wanted out of undercover government work, or whatever you two did." She never made him chose between the job and her. Even now in those dark times when she wanted to, if only to make a point, she didn't.

"Connor loved the kill. You ruined that for him."

That wasn't her husband. That wasn't the man she knew. The one that rescued and saved. "You don't know him at all."

"Says the woman who dumped him."

"That didn't happen."

Drake's hand swept across the Utah desert. "Looks like it."

"I was going back. Not right now, but eventually. I don't belong here." The truth hit her then. "But you knew that. That's why you had to take Connor out. You knew I would tell him and he would wonder how anything could go wrong with the shipments if you were watching over them."

"Being smart will be your downfall."

"Let her go, Drake."

At the sound of Connor's voice, Jana whipped around. She was so happy to see him, she almost didn't feel Drake's arm snake around her neck. Then he pulled her in tight and she had to grab his forearm to keep from choking.

"I see your skills are at a functional level." Drake shouted and it echoed in her ear. "What, is there a microphone on her? A tracker?"

His anger didn't stop Connor. He and Holt moved in slowly. Cam entered from the side, directly parallel to Drake.

"This is over," Connor said with a nod.

He didn't look at her. Stress pulled on his face and his body tightened as whatever emotion zipping around inside him took hold.

She'd seen this before and it soothed her rather than frightened her. This was warrior Connor. Just having him there had her sagging in relief against Drake.

"This has been going on long before now and eventually I'll set up somewhere else with someone other than Marcel, and move on." Drake gave Cam a quick glance. "You should stop moving unless you want to explain to Connor why his wife's blood is spilled all over the ground."

Connor lifted a hand. "Hold up."

"Speaking of loose ends, it would be helpful if you finished him off for me." Drake lifted his chin in the direction of the area behind Connor.

Until then she hadn't noticed the truck in the distance or Marcel tied up and walking in closer. He looked as if they'd dragged him outside the window. She knew that wasn't true, but she also knew Marcel had paid for some part of his role in this already.

"On your knees." Holt gave the order to Marcel and he obeyed.

"You're outnumbered here, Drake," Connor said.

Drake laughed and his breath blew against her hair. "Why do you think I'm alone?"

He said the words and fear tumbled right on top of Jana again. She'd begun to believe in the miracle. Connor never failed and he wouldn't this time. But there were other players and that could mean shots fired from anywhere.

She tried not to move anything except her eyes as she glanced around. Drake had been careful not to leave her a weapon. There was nothing within lunging range, not even a rock. That left the bags. She saw the guns inside one before he zipped it up. That bag had to have some weight. Question was if she could get the leverage she needed to swing it.

"Marcel?" Connor called out the man's name without turning around.

Marcel didn't hesitate. "He has a second-in-command type. Bruce. I haven't seen him in a few hours."

Jana scanned the area, looking for any signs of life. She took in every inch of red rock and dried tree and didn't see anyone. She'd settle for a snake at this point. Anything to draw Drake's attention and give Connor a clean shot.

"Only one, Drake? I guess that's because we killed everyone else."

"And you think your two are enough?" Drake nodded in Cam's direction as Drake angled his body tighter behind her. "Though I admit it's impressive this one survived the fire. Maybe you did learn something about leadership from me, Connor."

"I learned about being a man from my wife."

Jana's heartbeat triple timed. She hoped those weren't the last words she'd ever hear from her husband. Connor stood there out in the open, without a shield of any type, and it terrified her.

Yeah, she had to do something. Risk it all. If the bag pulled her shoulder out of joint or she got a shot in the side, so be it.

"Romantic." Drake's arm tightened. "The only question here is if I take her with me and make you spend your life hunting her down or if I take off and drop her from the sky. Preference?"

Connor didn't move. She knew the reaction was practiced…and killing him. But she would not go out like this. She would not be a victim or saddle the man she loved with the burden of watching her die.

Her choices put them here. He'd trained her and she would fight. He would know she pushed and shoved and did everything to come back to him.

Drake made a tsk-tsk sound. "Unfortunately, it's too late for anything else."

"No, it's not." Throwing all her weight, she nailed her head into his jaw. The thwack of pain had her stumbling and him swearing.

That worked in the movies. Not in real life. Pain seared across her temples. Stars buzzed in her head as she reached for the bag but her fingers refused to move. She couldn't grip and the daylight dimmed. She dropped down as the shots whizzed over her head. Her last thought was for Connor but even then the words wouldn't come.

CONNOR SAW HER DROP as her head lolled back. The hit knocked her out and part of him thought that was good. With her down, Holt and Cam unloaded into Drake. His body jerked and blood stained his shirt and head. After all the yelling and threats, he slid to the ground and his gun clanked against the helicopter as he went.

Connor didn't waste time on the man who'd betrayed him in every way possible. He and Cam crowded in on Jana. The world fell away and the idea of more bullets didn't matter. He wanted her up and to safety.

Placing two fingers on the side of her neck, Connor found a pulse and felt a whoosh of relief when her eyelids fluttered. "Come back to me, honey."

She inhaled sharply. "Are you okay?"

"We're all fine." His hands still shook and his brain stuttered on every other word, but none of that mattered. All he wanted was to hold her. Get her out of there and somewhere safe.

"I'm sorry." She whispered the word against his neck as he wrapped an arm around her and gathered her close.

The smallness of her voice made him ache. "For what?"

"Everything."

"Let's get you up." He got his legs under him with Cam's help and had a hand under her knees when the sharp crack of a single shot echoed from the distance.

It was the signal. Shane on lookout. He clearly saw something approaching.

They all turned. A single shooter walked straight toward them with Connor and Jana in his sights. Guns rose as Connor flattened her to the ground and rolled over her.

At the last second before the battle began, Marcel knocked into the guy. Stood up and ran, hitting him from the side and sending him reeling.

The man shot and Marcel went down with blood running out of his shoulder. But the attacker never got up. The team pumped enough artillery into him to make sure he never moved again.

Wobbling and woozy, Jana struggled to sit up. Connor didn't feel much better. Even without a head injury like hers, the past few minutes drained the energy from him but he found the strength to stand. He got an arm around her and guided her over to Marcel. Cam was already on his knees in the dirt, working on Marcel's injury as Holt talked with Shane over the satphone.

Marcel panted and the words came out of him in staccato beats. "Bruce. Down."

"That was him?" Connor asked.

"It's done." Marcel closed his eyes.

Connor took that to mean they'd gotten all of Drake's men. Also looked like Marcel gave up fighting. Not knowing whether Cam could pull the guy out of it and wanting to give some hope, Connor crouched down on the other side of him and let Cam do his work.

Battling his anger and the pulsing need to rip this guy apart, Connor picked up Marcel's hand and shook it. Those last few seconds meant something and Connor would honor those. "You saved her."

Marcel looked past Connor's shoulder. "I almost killed her."

Jana leaned her knees against Connor's back. He looked up and saw the cloudiness in her eyes had cleared.

"It's how you end that matters," she whispered.

Connor thought that said it all.

IT TOOK HOURS to clear the crime scene, which extended over several miles and throughout the desert. The police and emergency vehicles descended thanks to Shane's calls for help. They'd all been interviewed and checked out.

With Drake's job, a jurisdictional battle waged. Federal officers of all sorts showed up, each claiming the right to investigate and move in. Local officials didn't agree. Connor was left to help sort it out.

Jana spent longer than she wanted in a hospital bed while the doctor convinced Connor she didn't have a concussion. He did paperwork and the men joked. It all seemed so surreal.

So many dead men out in the desert. Men now in the morgue because of terrible decisions they'd made and their refusal to take any responsibility for their actions.

Except for Marcel. At the end he played the hero. He bounced into Bruce and got shot in return. Maybe it was a type of penance.

She'd forever see that final look in his eyes. Love and regret, pain and guilt. Forgetting the betrayal and fear would take longer. But she had a goal now and after hours in a hospital she was following through with it.

Not that Cam agreed with her tack.

He stepped in front of her, putting his body between her and the private plane. "Connor is going to kill us both."

The hangar smelled of fuel and people scurried around outside. She'd been in and out of small airports like this her entire life. They almost felt like home. Almost. "He's not."

"When he realizes you left the hospital and—"

She held up both hands. "I'll take full responsibility."

She had to do this. She needed Connor to understand she made the conscious choice. She wanted to go home.

Cam swore under his breath. "He's going to flip."

Footsteps thudded over her shoulder. She glanced up in time to see Connor walk in. Dressed in clean clothes and showered, he made her senses dance. Seeing him had her brain scrambling and her stomach twisting in anticipation.

The sure walk, the confident swagger. She loved it all.

And the scruff. It still outlined his chin. She'd try to convince him to keep that, at least for a short time.

He stopped right in front of her but saved a scowl for Cam. "I'm wondering why my wife is about to board a plane without telling me."

Cam cleared his throat. "I'll wait over there."

"Smart move." Connor shot Cam one last dark look. "We'll talk later."

"I figured." Cam's voice trailed off as he walked outside and into the sunshine.

She watched him go only to turn back and stare into the angry eyes of her husband. "Don't be mad at Cam. I forced him."

"He's a grown man."

"And I'm a grown woman." She waited for the verbal battle to begin. This time she'd win. Their marriage, their lives together, were too important not to.

Connor didn't disappoint. That scowl grew even more menacing. "Meaning?"

"I want to go home."

All the emotion ran out of his face and his expression went blank. "By yourself."

She knew that look was a bad sign. He'd blow…and soon. But she wasn't scared. He'd never hurt her and it was clear he'd never leave her, no matter how much either of them messed up.

"No, Connor."

His fury slipped as his eyes narrowed. "I don't understand what's happening here."

"I'm not going to let you do it. Storm in and take the blame for what happened with Drake." She put a hand against his chest, loving the feel of his muscles underneath.

He immediately covered her hand with his. "I didn't keep you safe."

There it was. The guilt and desperation that would always be between them. They bounced it back and forth, taking turns feeling bad about something. She planned to break that cycle now.

"You did. I left the protection of our home." And she had to take responsibility for that. After seeing adult men, someone like Drake with a lifetime of service behind him, not own up to being wrong, she'd vowed never to take that path.

Connor nodded. "Because I smothered you."

"Yes, you did." Pain moved behind his eyes and she rushed to wipe it out again. Her hand went to his chin and she caressed that stubbly skin. "But I still shouldn't have left. I should have somehow made you listen and understand. I gave up too fast, and I'm sorry for that."

His arms came around her. She sensed he wanted to gather her into a crushing bear hug but he settled for resting his arms loosely around her waist.

"I almost lost you today." The words sounded harsh, as if they were ripped out of him.

"I'm not going anywhere except home to our house, to our bed." She leaned in with her forehead resting against his and tried to believe how much she loved this man. "Do you know why?"

"Because your head injury made you loopy."

She smiled as she lifted her head. She caused him pain and pushed them apart, yet he didn't wallow. "Because I love you and don't want to be away from you."

His fingers tightened against her waist then relaxed again. "Wasn't that true when you walked out?"

"Yes."

He exhaled. "Not to sound ungrateful, but what's changed?"

Some small things that added up to everything. Some changes came from her and really were more about recognizing the things she had started to take for granted.

Seeing the way he looked at her. Feeling him against her as they made love. His strength, honor and loyalty.

"When you didn't put the tracker in my clothes, which I know was hard for you."

He rolled his eyes. "I nearly crushed the thing in my hand."

"But you didn't. You talked with me." Her palms found his cheeks. "We talked it out and I made the decision."

"Okay." He winced. "You know I may have tucked it in your pants if you said no, right? I want to take credit and be the bigger man and all that, but I don't know what I would have done if you fought me."

She loved his honesty and right now, after all the double-dealing and lies they'd seen, it meant even more. "Admittedly, we still have some work to do."

His hand went to her hair and he massaged the back of her head. "You know that I would do anything to keep you safe. That the idea of losing you is the only thing in this world that I cannot handle."

"And you know I feel the same way about you." That's the part she needed him to understand. "We are in this together. Both of us. Equally. I may not be a sharpshooter and can't crack a safe with a can opener, or whatever you do—"

"That's Shane."

"—but when it comes to our lives together and how we get through each day, we're equal. You worry about me and I worry about you."

"I get that." A few words, so simple and firm in their delivery.

She knew he meant them. "I just needed to know you understood that."

He pulled her in tighter until every curve of her body slipped into his. "For the record, even without the can opener skills, that was a pretty impressive head butt you did back there."

"You told me to use it as a last resort, and I was feeling pretty desperate." So much of what he'd taught her came rushing back when she needed it. He'd ingrained it in her. Maybe the strong-arm tactics annoyed her, but the skills stuck. "Point is, your training made a difference. Your surveillance made a difference. I think we can figure out a way to balance it all, but you have to meet me halfway."

"You're not the only one who learned something all these months, you know."

She hoped that was true. She was gambling everything on it. "What did you learn?"

He kissed her then. Leaned in and covered her mouth with his, passing and pressing until her hands went to his neck and her heart bounced against her ribs.

She smiled against his lips. "Well, I like that."

"You are a fierce, beautiful, strong and independent woman. I loved those things about you when I married you and I love them now." He kissed her nose and her cheeks. "I'm sorry I made you question any of that, that I didn't show you how I felt every day. But now I get that suppressing the things that make you who you are doesn't make either of us happy."

There it was. That little hiccup her heart did when he said something so perfect she wanted to tackle him and drag him off somewhere private. "And I'm sorry I didn't fight harder, that I left you at all."

He kissed her again. Quick but still so precious. "Forgiven."

She could see in his eyes he meant it. "So are you."

"Then you know what we need to do next."

He lifted her up until her toes barely touched the floor.

Even being tall he could make her feel cherished. “That smile promises something naughty.”

“We need to get back to Maryland first. If we do what I’m thinking on the plane, poor Cam might jump out.”

She bit back a laugh. “Then take me home.”

* * * * *

Read on for a sneak peek of
WEDDING AT CARDWELL RANCH
by New York Times *bestselling author*

B.J. Daniels

Part of the **CARDWELL COUSINS** *series.*

In Montana for his brother's nuptials, Jackson Cardwell isn't looking to be anybody's hero. But the Texas single father knows a beautiful lady in distress when he meets her.

"I'm afraid to ask what you just said to your horse," Jackson joked as he moved closer. Her horse had wandered over to some tall grass away from the others.

"Just thanking him for not bucking me off," she admitted shyly.

"Probably a good idea, but your horse is a she. A mare."

"Oh, hopefully she wasn't insulted." Allie actually smiled. The afternoon sun lit her face along with the smile.

He felt his heart do a loop-de-loop. He tried to rein it back in as he looked into her eyes. That tantalizing green was deep and dark, inviting, and yet he knew a man could drown in those eyes.

Suddenly, Allie's horse shied. In the next second it took off as if it had been shot from a cannon. To her credit, she hadn't let go of her reins, but she grabbed the saddle horn and let out a cry as the mare raced out of the meadow headed for the road.

Jackson spurred his horse and raced after her. He could hear the startled cries of the others behind him. He'd been riding since he was a boy, so he knew how to handle his horse. But Allie, he could see, was having trouble staying in the saddle with her horse at a full gallop.

He pushed his horse harder and managed to catch her, riding alongside until he could reach over and grab her reins. The horses lunged along for a moment. Next to him Allie started to fall. He grabbed for her, pulling her from her saddle and into his arms as he released her reins and brought his own horse up short.

Allie slid down his horse to the ground. He dismounted and dropped beside her. "Are you all right?"

"I think so. What happened?"

He didn't know. One minute her horse was munching on grass, the next it had taken off like a shot.

Allie had no idea why the horse had reacted like that. She hated that she was the one who'd upset everyone.

"Are you sure you didn't spur your horse?" Natalie asked, still upset.

"She isn't wearing spurs," Ford pointed out.

"Maybe a bee stung your horse," Natalie suggested.

Dana felt bad. "I wanted your first horseback-riding experience to be a pleasant one," she lamented.

"It was. It is," Allie reassured her, although in truth, she wasn't looking forward to getting back on the horse. But she knew she had to for Natalie's sake. The kids had been scared enough as it was.

Dana had spread out the lunch on a large blanket with the kids all helping when Jackson rode up, trailing her horse. The mare looked calm now, but Allie wasn't sure she would ever trust it again.

Jackson met her gaze as he dismounted. Dana was already on her feet, heading for him. Allie left the kids to join them.

"What is it?" Dana asked, keeping her voice down.

Jackson looked to Allie as if he didn't want to say in front of her.

"Did I do something to the horse to make her do that?" she asked, fearing that she had.

His expression softened as he shook his head. "You didn't do *anything*." He looked at Dana. "Someone shot the mare."

Someone is hell-bent on making Allie Taylor think she's losing her mind. Jackson's determined to unmask the perp. Can he guard the widowed wedding planner and her little girl from a killer with a chilling agenda?

HIEXP69770

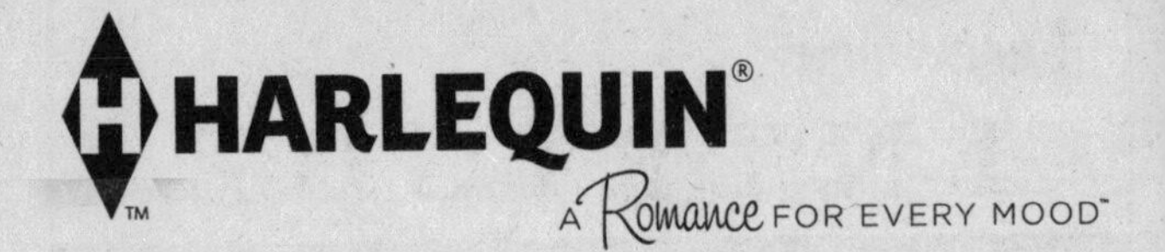
HARLEQUIN®
A Romance FOR EVERY MOOD™